Bloodhouse

Kenneth Cook was born i[n] ... [...] ey ... h[is] eleventh book. His work has been translated into several languages and his novel *Wake In Flight* was successfully filmed as *Outback*.

Kenneth Cook is concentrating on full-time writing under a three-year grant from the Australian Literature Board.

£2

KT-144-985

Kenneth Cook

Bloodhouse

Pan Books in association with
Heinemann

This novel was written on a
Commonwealth Literary Fellowship

First published in Great Britain 1974 by William Heinemann Ltd
This edition published 1977 by Pan Books Ltd,
Cavaye Place, London SW10 9PG
in association with William Heinemann Ltd
© Kenneth Cook 1974
ISBN 0 330 25193 7
Printed and bound in Great Britain by
Richard Clay (The Chaucer Press) Ltd, Bungay, Suffolk

for Patricia

Oft though wine has played the infidel
And done mine honour in men's eyes much wrong,
I often wonder what the vintners buy
One half so precious as the goods they sell

Counsel for the Prosecution:

Ladies and Gentlemen : The evidence you have heard has presented you with a scene of squalor, terror and confusion. The scene has been presented to you in fragments in the form of the evidence. It is for you to take these fragments, rejecting those you consider faulty, and piece them together into the true picture. On the basis of the picture which you honestly and objectively consider to be the true one, you must return your verdict.

It is not my function to secure a conviction. It is my function to help you to arrive at a true verdict. This is seldom a simple task, and in this case it is even more complex than usual. The complexity arises from the nature of the events, the conflict in evidence, and even in the matter of Law because in this case it is quite obvious that the accused had no intention of killing, or harming in any way the deceased. But that, as His Honour will tell you, is beside the point ... I shall say more about that later.

Let me now summarize the evidence you have heard, evidence which I will argue leads inevitably to your delivering a verdict of guilty, the evidence covering the events on Saturday the seventeenth of June last at the Hotel Calpe.

Counsel for the Defence:

My learned friend has rightly said that it is not his function to secure a conviction. It is his function, my function, the function of this court to arrive at the truth; and I will argue, I assure you, with heartfelt sincerity, that a realization of the truth in this case will lead you to a verdict of not guilty.

My friend has described the evidence you have heard as presenting a scene of squalor, terror and confusion. I would go further: it has presented you with a glimpse of hell, of a hell that is present in the very fabric of everyday civilized life.

His Honour will tell you, and I must agree, that you are bound by his instructions in the matter of Law. The evidence you have heard might lead you to bring in a verdict of guilty against persons who are not even on trial. His Honour will tell you, and I agree, that this is irrelevant, but His Honour will also tell you that if the picture of wretched degradation presented to you is so confused that you cannot say without a reasonable doubt that the accused is guilty, then you must return a verdict of not guilty.

In any event observed by human beings truth is to a certain extent in the eye of the beholder; that is why people of good will and integrity will give conflicting versions of the same event. Then again the truth is a matter of emphasis ... and this is very much the case in the events at the Hotel Calpe.

The Judge:

Ladies and Gentlemen: As learned counsel have so eloquently argued, the common man's understanding of murder is not necessarily the correct or only correct understanding. In Law a number of matters have to be proven before murder can be held to have been committed. These are:

The death of a human being.

That the deceased was a human being.

That the act or omission of the accused caused the death of the deceased.

That this act, or omission, was done with reckless indifference to human life, or with intent to kill, or with intent to inflict grievous bodily harm upon some person.

Or that this act, or omission, was done in an attempt to commit an act obviously dangerous to human life, or an act punishable by death, or a crime punishable by penal servitude for life.

It is further required to be proved, ladies and gentlemen, that this act or omission was malicious, or without lawful cause of excuse.

And finally, it must be proven that the deceased died of the wound or other injury given by the accused within a year and a day after he received it.

That is the Law, ladies and gentlemen, and it is for you to decide whether those proofs are available from the evidence given on the events of June the seventeenth at the Hotel Calpe.

The hotel was quite old by Australian standards, but a few years before somebody had taken it and remodelled it along the lines of what he thought was a Spanish drinking house. The outside was roughcast, painted white, and a few false arches had been put in over the doorways. There had been several canvas canopies over the windows, lending a touch of violent colour to the stark white building, but these had deteriorated in the sea air and had been replaced with metal awnings.

The Spanish-minded hotelier had not succeeded and the building had been through several hands in the past few years. The roughcast fell away in many places leaving the building looking as though it were covered in large sores. The metal awnings became tarnished and dingy. The inside bars were dark and impregnated with the stench of stale beer and the odours from the toilets which never seemed to work properly and were seldom cleaned. It was the haunt of local people only and they drank there because it was five miles to the next hotel. The tattered, depressed building became a sad monument to the misplaced ambitions of its various owners.

So the present owner had managed to buy it quite cheaply. He was a man of some commercial vision and an acute notion of the requirements of twentieth-century youth. He had the roughcast restored and repainted. The inside bars were stripped, the walls covered with metal and plastic, and the floors with carpet. The bars were remodelled and given appropriate names: 'The Bull Room' and the

'Lovers' Lounge' and the 'Surfers' Bar'. The decrepit toilets were completely retiled and the doors labelled 'Guys' and 'Gulls' respectively. The problems of sewage disposal were solved efficiently by installing an illegal pipe in the septic tank and running all waste matter into the sea a few yards out from the shore. This tended to make much of the beach unusable but it was no part of the hotelier's design to encourage people to loiter on the sands.

The walls were decorated with the accoutrements of those who use the sea for sport and work: surf-boards, underwater masks, snorkels, rope, fishing net and so forth, all placed high on the walls where they were well out of the reach of the patrons.

Centrally in the main lounge the hotelier had a stage installed, equipped with an amplification system of such power that any sound projected through it could be heard some miles away on a still day.

To supplement the proposed sounds from the stage a huge and glittering juke-box was set up at the other end of the lounge. The juke-box too was capable of producing enormous volumes of sound although it could not compete with the stage amplification system. To ensure that no drinking would ever be done in silence a taped music system was connected to every public room in the hotel and a large television set was let into the wall in the bar which, it was expected, would still be used by the local people.

The renovations complete, the hotelier installed his last piece of equipment – a publican to run the place, a man with long experience and great affection for his trade. The hotelier then went away, content with his labours and, because he was a very rich man, happy to wait for years if need be to see their fruits.

The publican's name was Mick. Above the door of the

hotel, as required by law, the drinker could discover that Mick's second name was Buchanan and that he was licensed to sell fermented and spirituous liquors, but nobody ever knew him as anything but Mick.

Mick was a man of immense size and unbelievable energy. His face would have been ugly had it been human, but to describe Mick as ugly would have been as incongruous as describing an ape as ugly. His visage was hideous, but had a certain quality of permanence as though it had been deliberately designed that way for some obscure but definite purpose. He had a wide, slack mouth and fat lips which wobbled in rhythm with the flesh that hung in pouches under his eyes and about his chin. His eyes were pale and bulged slightly and in their setting of pale pouched flesh looked like two small poached eggs. His hair was thick and curly, greying now in his fortieth year, but it would have been his only attractive feature had he not kept it so short that it stuck out around his head like steel wool.

Mick was well over six feet tall and his body was the body of a heavy football player to which had been added layer after layer of fat in thicknesses appropriate to the portions of the body to which they were applied. Everything about Mick was fat. He had fat fingers, fat legs, fat arms, a fat nose and fat ears, as well as the enormous symmetrically fat body. His awesome appearance was augmented by his intense energy. He always moved quickly, almost at a trot, and it was a brave drinker who did not politely make way when Mick, solid and irresistible as a bull, came jogging through the bars.

He spoke in sharp, rapid staccato style that would have indicated nervousness in a man to whom it was possible to attribute nerves, but with Mick speed of speech was a form of efficiency and Mick was very efficient.

From the time he took the job as publican he was never

known to take a day off or leave the hotel for more than a couple of hours.

'Mick's life is hotels,' his wife, Jenny, would say : 'I knew that before I married him. There's no point in standing between a man and what he wants in life, so I go along with him.'

'Going along with him' meant loyally serving in the bar, attending to the books, lending a hand in the kitchen and being Mick's mentor, soulmate and comfort in bed. Jenny was as fat as Mick, but she was very short, a little under five feet from her fat little feet to the very blonde hair that she wore in tight curls around her head. Her small bright brown eyes were always merry and she bounced around the hotel like a good humoured, animated pudding. She was almost as energetic as Mick and, seen from the rear trotting through the hotel, the two of them resembled an elephant with a calf at its side.

Jenny's blonde hair seemed to be natural, and her complexion was very fair. She enhanced this with a heavy application of powder and from a distance the pudding illusion was increased to include a dusting of icing sugar on the top.

Mick's complexion had suffered from years in hotels, but a relic of some outdoor past had ingrained itself in his skin and he was a sallow, brownish colour, rather like the colour of stale beer.

They were a bizarre looking couple, but their very appearance lent them a semblance of human personality. They were the travesties that proved the perfection of the norm and their grotesqueness made them superficially lovable, concealing the fact that they were as lethal as tuberculosis bacillus.

Mick and Jenny had been married for twenty years, but had had no children. Instead they housed a succession of cats to which they appeared quite devoted. The latest incumbent on their affections was a monstrous tom-cat called Mol. The name was bestowed because of a mistake about the cat's sex when it was first acquired as a kitten to replace a tabby which had been squashed under a barrel of beer being unloaded from a truck. Mol's true sex had become apparent as time passed – more than one customer remarked that decency required the animal be provided with trousers – but the name stuck.

Despite a certain ferociousness of aspect Mol was a very amiable cat; possibly its natural feline dispositions had been softened by the affection with which it was treated by Mick and Jenny. It daily ate several meals which would have kept a human family of three or four in reasonable health, and slept with Mick and Jenny in the double bed which they shared in one of the top rooms of the hotel. Jenny had been seen dressing the acquiescent cat in the doll's clothes, but it never appeared in the public rooms of the hotel in any other than its naked state.

Mick, Jenny and Mol had been in the hotel less than six months before the perspicacity of the hotelier began to pay off. In its early days the hotel had suffered financially because of its distance from Sydney, but the bursting city boundaries had bulged out towards it and suddenly people discovered that it was not all that long a drive from their homes. Because of a technicality based on its distance from the Metropolitan area the hotel was legally entitled to open for Sunday trading. It was in a pleasant spot on a narrow neck of land running out into the sea, so that drinkers who cared to look out of windows on either side of the building could see the surf breaking on the beach below, and to the north and south the splendid cliffs of the New South Wales coast.

A couple of hours' drive from the city, it became popular

amongst those whose pleasure it is on a Sunday to drive for the morning in a continuous stream of traffic, sit in a crowded hotel for several hours consuming beer then, befuddled, to join the stream of traffic towards their homes. The magnificent views were seldom observed except by those who, dropping in for a drink, were appalled by the crowded, noisy, smoke-filled bars and immediately went away again.

But those who stayed liked the place. They liked the decor. They liked the piped music. They liked the juke-box, and they liked the mind-blasting band which Mick had installed on the stage on week-end afternoons and evenings. The band was the cheapest Mick could find consistent with his requirements. His methods of audition were simple. He allowed the various groups to play briefly through the amplification system and chose the one which could produce the longest, loudest, continuous sound without losing the mind-blasting thud of rhythm. Mick's musical tastes were curiously in time with his customers'.

The band, the decor and the personalities of Mick and Jenny gave the place a reputation which spread quickly. In the past few years suburbs had sprung up far from the centre of Sydney and the hotel was within the range of customers who, while not strictly speaking living far enough away to qualify as 'bona fide' travellers, nevertheless took advantage of lax police supervision to enjoy its facilities on Sundays. These people, victims of a town planning system which forced them to live in areas of unremitting dreariness, found the hotel to their liking and because they lived close enough became regular nightly customers.

Mick, who was a brilliant publican where profitability is a criterion of brilliance, saw what was happening and exploited it. He engaged bands for Wednesday and Friday nights as well as the week-end and put two more even bigger and louder juke-boxes in the other bars. As the proportion of very young people among his customers increased he offered a greater variety of 'mixed drinks' with startling names like 'Devil's Breath', 'Bedsheets', 'Belly-strokes' and 'Gentle Joan', whose main characteristics were that they were very sweet, made from very cheap alcohol and were very expensive. Mick encouraged groups to make the hotel their headquarters and several bands of water-skiers, motor-cyclists and drag-car racers met there fairly regularly.

In all, the hotel became 'a place to go' for many of the disenchanted within a radius of twenty miles or more. The hotel prospered mightily. Mick's percentage of the profits was enormous. The hotelier, surprised and gratified at the early success of his inspiration congratulated himself on the choice of Mick as publican and set about applying his profits to establishing another hotel in the same vein on the other side of Sydney.

The people of the small fishing village which the hotel had originally served observed the changes apathetically. The local tradespeople vaguely felt that the hotel's success must bring business to the community. The few fishermen and farmers who still survived in the district did their drinking in the public bar and complained about the noise, but they still did their drinking in the public bar.

Another race of men were moving into the district now; real estate agents, builders, professional people seeking a haven. They were sometimes seen in the hotel when the band wasn't playing. Their children were often seen there when it was.

A few old men who had once been fishermen liked to sit on the seats outside the hotel in the mornings, making a little beer go a long way. Mick let them stay there in the mornings, but in the afternoons he chased them away to make room for people who drank their beer more quickly. They complained and they cursed Mick, but they came back next morning because they had been gathering there for many years now and it was hard to change.

The atmosphere of prosperity made very little difference to Mick or Jenny. Because they were good at their job they had never wanted for money. The fact that they now had much more money than they needed was a matter of small moment. Mick was an artist in the sense that his creation provided its own reward in terms other than money. All he wanted to do was to run a hotel successfully. While he was doing that there was nothing that life could give him, or take away from him. He delighted in the mechanics of his art – the giving of short measure, pouring cheap whisky into bottles carrying noble brands of Scotch, the ruthless suppression of dishonesty in the staff, the violent quelling of obstreperous customers, the persuading of customers by forceful service to drink too much and, when they had, to induce them to drink more.

Mick lived undeviatingly by the unwritten motto of the Australian publican – Never refuse to sell a man a drink unless you think he's going to break the furniture. He had his art, and he had Mol and Jenny to love.

All Jenny wanted was to be able to work with Mick and look after Mol. Because both had exactly what they wanted from life they could be held to be happy. Mol always seemed content to satiation.

'Where's Mol?' said Mick one Saturday morning as he was giving the bar in the lounge a perfectionist's polish before opening time while Jenny counted change into one of the tills.

'He was still in bed ten minutes ago,' said Jenny, pausing thoughtfully. 'Will I go and see if he's still there?'

Mick pondered. He couldn't work happily unless he knew the cat was safe. Still, it was ridiculous to worry too much. If Jenny had seen him in the bed ten minutes ago he was probably still there.

'No. Let him sleep in,' said Mick, recommencing his vigorous polishing. 'The old fellow was out last night. I think he might be a bit shagged.'

'Oh, Mick,' said Jenny, who in the course of one day heard more obscenities than most women heard in a lifetime, but nevertheless always reacted coyly whenever Mick made the most mildly suggestive remark.

'Well, you don't think he carries those bloody great balls for nothing, do you?' said Mick. His staccato speech went with a deadpan expression and the combination of these with some slightly outrageous remark gave him a reputation as a wit.

'Oh, Mick,' said Jenny.

'Get out with you,' said Mick. 'You know as well as I do he's the father of half the kittens in the district.'

'Oh he is not. Poor old Mol.'

'Poor old Mol me eye. Wish I had had his luck.'

'Stop it, Mick,' said Jenny.

'Actually I ought to,' said Mick. 'Ought to have him cut. Be doing the decent thing by the neighbours.'

It was an old conversation. Both took some pride in Mol's reputed potency.

'I'll see you cut first, you old brute,' said Jenny.

Mick laughed, or made the sound that passed for laughter with him: a sharp, coughing grunt. He skipped over to Jenny and dug his fingers into her enormous rump well below her spine.

'I'm safe enough there. That's one thing you wouldn't do, isn't it? You know what's good for you, don't you, old girl?'

'Oh, Mick,' said Jenny, disengaging his hand and gently slapping it. She glanced around to see whether any of the staff had observed the display of connubial affection. She would have literally blushed if any had. She had a great capacity for blushing, her skin went bright pink under the layer of powder. In fact she cultivated it because she found it made people laugh to see her illuminate like a frosted light globe and Jenny liked to make people laugh.

'It's all right. No one's looking,' said Mick. 'Anyhow, it'd be no news to them after the row we made last night.' The bed which Mick and Jenny shared was old and given to creaking and under their combined vast weights was inclined to give audible evidence of any movement on the mattress.

Jenny blushed and Mick laughed.

'Bet that was why old Mol spent the night out,' said Mick, finishing with the bar and turning his attention to the beer taps. 'Bet he couldn't stand the noise.'

He looked to see whether his chaffing was deepening the colour in Jenny's cheeks. It was.

'Oh, Mick,' said Jenny, reduced to helplessness and holding her hands over her face.

'Or maybe he just got jealous and went out to find a bit of his own.' Mick's laughter increased in volume and speed so that the flesh on his face began to wobble sideways rather than up and down as it did when he was talking.

Jenny took one hand away from her suffused face to slap at her husband's chest.

'Mick! Stop it at once,' she giggled.

Suddenly Mick turned serious and began to worry. The bar would be open soon and business would be brisk even early on a Saturday morning. There wouldn't be much time to go looking for Mol later and he didn't want to feel uneasy all the morning.

'You're sure old Mol's still in bed,' he said. 'He's usually down by now.'

Jenny looked tenderly at Mick.

'Are you worried, pet, would you like me to go and look?'

'Would you mind, old girl? I do worry about that cat.'

'I know you do. All right I'll go and look. But you're worrying for nothing, you old goose.'

'Thanks, Jenny. And listen, as you go through send young Mary in will you. I want to straighten her out on that affair last night.'

'All right, Mick.'

Jenny rolled away across the carpeted lounge. Mick waited until she was in the doorway then called out: 'And while you're there you'd better do what you can to tighten up the springs on that bed.'

'Oh, Mick,' said Jenny, clapping her hands over her ears, looking around to see whether the staff had heard and never admitting in her own mind the fact that if the bed noises had disturbed anybody the previous night it had been the first time for many months, and there hadn't been very much noise anyway.

Counsel for the Prosecution:

My learned friend called a great deal of evidence of the mere mechanics of hotel life. Some of this evidence has been derogatory to various persons, and my friend argues that it has been necessary to bring this evidence because it is pertinent to his case. His Honour will instruct you in the Law, but it is obvious that it is John Verdon who is on trial here, nobody else. In any case there has been much conflict in the evidence brought and inasmuch as my friend relies on this evidence to support his arguments, I would suggest that his reliance is misplaced. In other words I am saying that what you heard is not necessarily true, and that even if it were, it would not affect the issue. My friend argues otherwise and His Honour will instruct you further in the matter.

But this then, loosely, was the scene on which the accused, John Verdon, was to appear later in the day. A scene, in my interpretation of it and, I suggest, the interpretation of the normal man of commonsense, a scene of ordinary preparation for the day's business by two people engaged in catering for the recreational needs of a section of the community.

Now, what of the actions of the accused: on his own statement he spent the morning at work . . .

Counsel for the Defence:

It is necessary to understand the full situation that applied that day if you are to be able to discern the truth in the maelstrom of events. Because in this case the truth is separate from the events. The truth lies in the degree of knowledge and understanding of the accused. Even if he committed the acts suggested by part of the evidence, it is possible that his understanding of the situation led him to perform those acts in perfect good faith. If you recognize the possibility, and I suggest you must on the evidence, you will bring in a verdict of not guilty. And I remind you that he is charged with murder, nothing else. Whatever else you may think he did is beside the point. He is charged with murder. You must be convinced that he committed murder, or you must acquit him.

As you heard, John Verdon began that day at his place of work ...

The Judge:

Some of the matters required to be proven in this case are not in dispute.

It is accepted that a human being died as a result of the injury inflicted within the required time.

What is in dispute is whether the act of the accused caused the death of the deceased.

It is plain, as Counsel has said, that there is no question of the accused having intended to kill the deceased. What has to be decided, and it is your onerous duty to decide, is whether or not an act of reckless indifference to human life by the accused led to the death of the deceased.

Alternatively you have to decide whether or not an act of the accused, obviously dangerous to human life, led to the death of the deceased, or whether the accused in attempting to kill someone else, caused the death of the deceased.

Should you come to the conclusion that no action on the part of the accused led to the death of the deceased, you will return a verdict of not guilty.

Should you come to the conclusion that some act of the accused did lead to the death of the deceased, you must then consider whether or not such an act was malicious or without lawful cause or excuse.

Learned Counsel has argued that the state of mind of the accused is relevant, and so it is: with several limiting factors about which I will speak later.

Evidence has been brought about the accused's occupation and this evidence, I am to instruct you, you must regard as irrelevant. The accused's occupation is a normal, recognized function in society and, with respect to learned Counsel, I must deplore the introduction of evidence on this occupation in the manner in which it was introduced. There is no reason to suppose that a man of John Verdon's occupation is more given to violence than other men, and in any case a disposition to violence is not a proof, not even substantive evidence, of violent action.

Therefore you will remove from your mind any consideration of the work of the accused . . .

John Verdon moved forward on the balls of his feet, swung the sledgehammer effortlessly over his right shoulder and let it fall with just a slight drive of his arms so that the hammer did most of the work.

The point of the hammer head crunched cleanly into the skull of the steer with a sound and a sensation that Verdon felt down to his loins.

The stunned beast collapsed and as the side of the chute fell away, rolled on to the concrete floor a couple of feet below. Verdon's mate, Bob Harris, hooked its legs to a chain and automatically the steer was hauled into the air upside down. It began to revive, tearing at the air with its forelegs, vainly jerking against the chain holding its hind legs. It let out a terrified bellow which ended in a wet gurgle as Harris cut its throat and let the great rush of dark, almost black, blood flood out on to the floor. The forelegs kept thrashing.

The steer's lungs were still trying to draw air until the chain carried it to the next stage of the meatworks where someone cut off its head.

The carcase went on around the line while fifty knives attacked the still hot flesh, dismembering it while the heart convulsively beat until someone tore it out.

John Verdon waited casually as the next steer stumbled up the chute. He operated the door which let it into the killing pen, then began his swing with the hammer. The beast slipped on some slime on the floor of the pen and the hammer missed. It smashed away a horn and thudded into the animal's shoulder. The beast bellowed and went down on its knees.

'Fuck it,' said Verdon, and looked around to see whether the foreman had noticed the bungled job. Not that it would have mattered. Verdon's reputation with the hammer was such that even one clearly careless mistake would not have tarnished it. This incident, which was unavoidable, was irrelevant, but Verdon was very jealous of his reputation. He liked killing and he liked to be known as a good killer. Most days he put his hammer through the skulls of a hundred steers without a mishap, and he hated it when something went wrong. It just didn't feel good unless he killed properly.

Verdon grabbed the electric rod and jabbed at the steer until it stood up. He swung the hammer again, but the beast was still moving erratically. The hammer caught it on the head, but it wasn't a clean blow. Verdon could tell it wasn't a clean blow as much from the feeling in his loins as any- thing else. There had been no satisfaction in it. But it had been enough to drop the beast and now it wallowed in the bottom of the pen.

Verdon opened the side of the chute. The steer rolled out on to the floor and immediately tried to get up. It slipped and crashed in the blood of its fellows and Harris quickly hooked its legs to the chain and it was hauled up, bellowing and thrashing frantically. Harris cut its throat.

'Watch it, mate,' he called amiably to Verdon. 'Don't want 'em running around down here you know.'

Verdon grunted. It was fair comment. A half-stunned steer on the floor below could be dangerous to the man on the chain. It was a fair comment, but Verdon didn't like it. He looked down at the long line of steers moving up the chute to the killing pen. Many of them were bellowing and all were turning their heads from side to side as though mystified at the stench of blood that flooded the air of the meatworks.

Verdon opened the killing pen and the next beast staggered in. Verdon took a little more trouble this time and the beast dropped cleanly, abruptly. The side of the chute opened and the beast rolled out, already quite dead. Verdon grinned down at Harris.

There was some hold-up in the chute and Verdon glanced around the meatworks. Another thirty or so kills and he could knock off. The animals he had already killed that morning were in various stages of dissection. The last one had already lost its head and been disembowelled, the steaming mass of blue and yellow intestines slopping into a moving tray that bore them away for conversion into various items of use to man.

Harris, his thigh boots wet and his apron saturated with blood, was waiting for the next kill. Expert knives all around the floor were slashing at the carcases and over to the right, like crows around a corpse, a group on the flaying floor were tearing off the brown skins and consigning the white and bloodless bodies to further dissection.

On a mobile tray just near the killing pen the detached heads of the animals were moving along an assembly line. They had been flayed and they were white and ghost-like; their tongues had been cut out, but so recently had they died that their eyeballs were still moving, twitching from side to side, a mournful parody of life above the bloodied lips and nostrils.

Verdon, prime mover in this process whereby man's meat went through the process of being converted into the more acceptable form in which it is presented at the butcher's shop, flexed his shoulder muscles and waited for the next animal to come through.

'Come on, you fuckers,' he said aloud, as the blockage

was cleared and the long, brown, swaying line began moving towards his hammer.

It had been a hard week and he was working overtime. Not that he minded, but he'd be glad when he finished work. He was a small man with superb muscular development and he didn't tire easily, but now he needed a beer. The Saturday overtime had disrupted his normal week-end routine, which was to stuff himself with beer from eleven o'clock on Saturday morning until he collapsed some time on Sunday morning and then, when he woke, to keep on stuffing himself with beer until he collapsed on Monday morning. The first few beasts he hit a few hours later on Monday morning were sometimes a bit mangled before they died, but he soon got his eye in.

But now it was Saturday morning and by rights he should have already started pouring in the beer. He was feeling irritable.

'Come on, you fuckers,' he shouted aloud as the beast came into the pen. He felled it neatly with rather more force than he normally used.

The rest of the morning's kill went smoothly except for the second last beast which raised its snout to bellow just as the hammer fell. The hammer caught it full on the teeth and smashed its jaws. It went down and wouldn't get up again, thrashing and bellowing on the floor of the killing pen.

'Let him down, Johnny, I'll fix him,' called Harris.

'Fuck it,' said Verdon. He knew it wasn't his fault, but this was two bad kills in the morning and he didn't like it. He prodded the steer with the electric rod, but that only made its thrashing wilder. He tried to hit it on the head with the hammer, but he couldn't get a decent swing with the animal laying on its side.

Enraged at the creature's failure to co-operate in its own

death, Verdon leaped into the killing pen and stood on the heaving body. He still couldn't get a decent swing at it, but at least he could reach its head. Holding the hammer half way along the handle he pounded at the steer until it finally subsided. Verdon climbed out of the pen and let the steer drop out.

'Christ, you fucked up this one, Johnny,' observed Harris as he hooked the beast's legs.

When that particular head was flayed and on the assembly line, its smashed skull and splintered jaws gave it an erratic appearance amongst the austere and ghostly skulls and twitching eyeballs.

The kill ended and the animals went on to become steak, sausages, tripe, liver, kidneys, black pudding and tongue to nourish the world of man, the most voracious carnivore of all time.

John Verdon, the instrument of a society which needed its meat but didn't have to kill it, went to the showers in a foul mood. Inasmuch as his work gave him pleasure apart from the reward of money, he too was an artist and faulty execution distressed him in a way he couldn't explain.

It never occurred to him and his friend Harris to discuss whether or not they were going to the hotel. Of course they were.

Counsel for the Prosecution:

Detailed evidence of the happenings of that day have been given by various members of the staff of the hotel. Much of this has been challenged by the defence and, admittedly, much of it is contradictory. It is for you to sort out in your own minds which is true, deliberately false or merely mistaken.

Counsel for the Defence:

I suggest that it is difficult to believe anything you have
heard from the staff of the hotel or the customers. I suggest
that the whole of the case for the prosecution is based on
the statements of people who are so intrinsically unreliable
that you must reject them.

The Judge:

Another point for your consideration is that the Law provides that no person shall be guilty of murder if he kills another person by misfortune only.

Counsel for the defence has argued that this point could well apply should you come to the conclusion that the accused did in fact commit an act which lead to the death of the deceased.

In that case the reliability of certain witnesses as to the events at that hotel is of paramount importance, and this reliability has been challenged.

'Mol's still sound asleep. I told you he was,' said Jenny.

'Oh good,' said Mick. 'Did you tell Mary I wanted her?'

'I'm here, Mick,' said Mary, a diminutive creature who for the moment had been hidden by Jenny's bulk.

'Just come in here for a minute, Mary,' said Mick, his demeanour serious. All his staff called him Mick, but none meant or showed any disrespect in his presence. His serious manner now made the girl Mary nervous. She was a casual in the reception office who occasionally helped out behind the bar. She was a pleasant enough looking girl who had been born and educated locally. Until she'd started working at the hotel she'd had a job in a hardware store. She hadn't liked that job any more than she liked working in the hotel, but she badly wanted a permanent job in the hotel. When her parents asked why, she said she liked the work. When her friends asked her why, she said she liked the social life. By which she meant the many and varied offers of intercourse that were made to her by men well-flown with drink. She hadn't accepted any yet, but one day she felt sure some nice young man would come in and want to take her out, and perhaps he wouldn't be drunk when he asked.

Mick led her into the office and began to talk quickly and earnestly.

'Now listen, Mary, just tell me what you saw here last night.'

'You mean the fight, Mick?'

'Just tell me what you saw.'

'Well, there was a fight. It was two fellows and they

started fighting in the lounge, and, well, you stopped it.'

'Is that all you saw?'

'Well, as they were going out one of them fell over and the other one dragged him out.'

'Which one fell over?'

'The one you hit, Mick.'

Mick paused to allow for emphasis on his next words.

'I didn't hit anybody, Mary.'

Mary looked up into the gross face and the poached egg eyes peering earnestly at her. She was aware she was being told something, but, as she wasn't all that bright a child, didn't know what.

'Oh,' she said uncertainly, 'I thought you hit one on the neck with that stick you keep behind the bar.'

'I didn't, Mary. I keep that stick behind the bar as a threat. You've never seen me take it out.'

Mary, who had seen him take it out at least four times in the past week, marvelled at this.

Mick observed that he was being too subtle.

'Look, Mary, one of those fellows is in hospital. He's got concussion.'

'Was that the one you ... you didn't ... did ...?' Mary gave up.

'The police may want to know something about it.'

'I see,' said Mary, who didn't.

'Now in a hotel anything that happens in the premises is the concern of the publican, do you understand?'

'Yes ...' said Mary doubtfully.

'So if two young fellows have a fight and one is hurt in the pub then that's my business, understand?'

'Yes.'

'But if they go outside and have a fight that's got nothing to do with me.'

'I see,' said Mary.

Mick looked down at her doubtfully.

'Mary,' he said. 'You want a permanent job here, don't you?'

'Yes, Mick.' Mary looked up hopefully. Perhaps that was what this was all about.

'Well if you want a permanent job you have to know something about pub work.'

'Of course. Yes, Mick, I see that.'

'All right. Now if the police ask you, what will you tell them about that fight last night?'

Mary gaped at him. She knew now what he was getting at, but couldn't for the life of her think what he wanted her to say. She knew he didn't want her to tell the truth, that she had seen him walk up behind a drunken youth and smash his ebony waddy hard down on his neck, but she could not form the lie that was expected of her. It wasn't that she wouldn't, simply that she couldn't.

She goggled. The fat of Mick's face resolved itself into a look of displeasure. Inspiration came to Mary.

'I'll say whatever you want me to say, Mick.'

Mick sighed. He didn't want to have to spell it out. But it would have to be that way.

'All right,' he said. 'What you saw was a fight between those two fellows. I spoke to them and they left. That's all. Got it?'

'They had a fight and you spoke to them and they left,' said Mary faithfully. 'Yes, I've got that, Mick, I understand now.'

'Do you?' said Mick thoughtfully. 'Good.' It didn't matter much. The local police sergeant understood the situation and was very tolerant, but he had to have some help as well as the occasional cash encouragement.

'Is there a chance of a permanent job, Mick?' said Mary, aware now that the discussion was over.

'We'll see,' said Mick heavily. 'We'll see.' He walked away, resolving to replace Mary as soon as somebody remotely presentable turned up who would work for the same wages.

'Hullo, Mol,' he said, stopping to stroke the great cat which rubbed itself against his legs. 'Decided to crawl out of the cot did you, you old devil? Come on and Dad'll get you something to eat. What do you feel like, eh? Drop of milk, bit of fish? You could probably do with some liver after last night.'

Jenny, who was behind the bar serving the early drinkers, said fondly to one on her customers, 'Dear me, he does spoil that cat, treats it like a child he does.'

The customer, a real estate agent suffering from a hang-over, grimaced politely.

Counsel for the Prosecution:

In reaching your verdict you will be obliged to consider at length the evidence of the youth Peter Watts. If you accept his statement as true, then I suggest you must bring a verdict of guilty.

Counsel for the Defence:

To convict a man of murder on the evidence of a boy of the established character and mental calibre of Peter Watts would be an act of utter irresponsibility.

The Judge:

If the accused brought about the death of the deceased by an act which followed by pure misfortune from a lawful act, then he is innocent. If he brought about the death of the deceased by an act which followed from an unlawful act, then he is guilty of murder. Here lies the crux of the case for the prosecution and for the defence. If you accept the version of events as told by John Verdon, then John Verdon could be held to be innocent. If you accept the version as told by Peter Watts, then John Verdon could be held to be guilty. You must therefore in your deliberations give great consideration to the evidence of Peter Watts.

Peter Watts stood naked in front of the mirror in his bedroom and wondered what to wear. He looked with sympathy and affection but no great satisfaction at the skinny frame of his seventeen-year-old body. The narrow shoulders and the girlish, too-big hips embarrassed him. He turned sideways and pulled in his stomach. That was better. If he could always stand like that, and only be seen from the side, he'd look good naked. Not that he looked bad, he thought, because he couldn't think ill of himself, but he looked better from the side. He began to brush his long, fair hair, studying his face intently. It was a good face, he decided, if he kept his lips tight so that his mouth didn't sag. But he knew he often forgot and went around with his mouth gaping open. It was like his stomach. If he remembered and kept it in tight it looked all right, but he kept on forgetting and usually went around with his stomach sagging and his mouth gaping. Today he'd keep his stomach in and his lips drawn tight and he'd try to look at the girls sideways so that they'd only see his profile. Although that wasn't all that important because he had some good new gear, he remembered with pleasure, and probably today he'd do all right. It was only if he got his gear off that it would matter. The thought of getting his gear off automatically brought his eyes down to his genitals and his hand strayed to his groin as though to encompass the warm sensation that grew there.

He was uneasy about his genitals if he allowed himself to imagine them specifically in action. He thought often enough about coitus, almost all the time in fact, but always in a sexual fantasy in which somehow he seemed older than he was, with a beautiful body and the girls groaned and writhed and begged for more. In reality, if he had allowed himself to, he might have doubted that he was capable of giving them anything, much less more.

He finished brushing his hair, satisfied that it had a good sheen. That was the one aspect of his appearance with which he was totally satisfied; thick, fair hair that fell down in graceful curls to his shoulders.

He went to the drawer of his dressing table and took out his new shirt, a heavy half-silk creation with colourful embroidery and a cut around the shoulders that made them puff rather than cling to the contours of the body. The shirt felt good on his skin as he slipped it over his head and for a moment he stood looking at himself in the mirror again. But the shirt hanging down to his thighs accentuated the skinniness of his legs and he turned away to find his jeans. He thought about the vivid underpants he'd bought last month, but he'd heard a man say in the pub that he never wore underpants because they were only something else to get off before you could get into action, and decided against them. He pulled on the jeans, glimpsing and rejecting the spots on his bottom, and tucked in the shirt.

That was good he thought, as he buckled the wide leather belt. The skin-tight jeans narrowed his hips and the loose-cut shirt widened his shoulders. He was a good-looking fellow. He turned sideways and that looked even better. Today would be great. One last brush of his hair and he set out for the day's adventure.

In the kitchen of the three-bedroom fibro house, Peter's father was mending a toaster.

'Christ Almighty,' he said. 'Where did you get that shirt?'

'Bought it,' said Peter, noncommittally. He'd stopped being nervous of his father ever since he started earning more as a builder's labourer than his father earned from his job as a linesman with the PMG.

'You look like a bloody queer,' said the father, a short, squat hairy man who greatly doubted his son's masculinity.

'Pity,' said Peter. He had often been accused of being a homosexual. He hadn't liked it at first, but lately it had become a kind of distinction. Like his clothes and his hair, the reputation of being queer added something to his personality, or in fact perhaps gave him a personality. He knew he wasn't homosexual, or didn't think he was, and didn't much care anyway.

'Where are you going?'

'Out with the boys.'

The father grunted. He'd long since lost any power over his son, but thought he ought to have it.

'Couldn't you put some bloody shoes on?'

Peter grinned. The beautiful clothes with no shoes were the thing, and the old man couldn't see it.

He didn't answer and sauntered out, picking up his motor-cycle helmet from the kitchen cupboard.

'You'd better be back to dinner. I don't want your mother cooking you a meal for nothing.'

'Tell her to put it in the oven,' said Peter.

'And keep out of that bloody pub. I'll get the police on to that bastard if he serves grog to you kids.'

It was a ritual and Peter ignored it. He kicked the starter on his grossly overpowered motor-cycle and roared away towards the hotel.

Counsel for the Defence:

It is an established fact that there was no previous association between Peter Watts and John Verdon. They had not seen each other before that day. They did not in fact exchange a word until the very end of that day, until they actually were face to face in the last short act of the drama which culminated in tragedy. And yet the prosecution suggests that intense animosity towards Peter Watts was John Verdon's prime motive.

Counsel for the Prosecution:

As men and women of the world you will know that hatred, like love, can arise instantaneously in the human heart, and for very little reason.

The Judge:

The defence case is that John Verdon's actions towards Peter Watts were prompted by lawful reasons. The prosecution's case is that the actions were prompted by malicious reasons. It is precisely the nature of those reasons that you must determine.

John Verdon was already half drunk by the time Peter Watts arrived at the hotel. Like so many very heavy drinkers he had a low tolerance to alcohol and after four or five beers could have been considered technically intoxicated. He was sitting at a table with his floor-mate Bob Harris. The two men looked strangely alike. They both were in their early twenties, rather small but very muscular, with unkempt hair of various colours but of uniform neck length. Both wore jeans and shirts and heavy boots. After half an hour's rapid and fairly silent drinking they were becoming talkative.

It was early afternoon and the hotel trade was beginning to build up. There were twenty or thirty locals in the public bar solemnly ingesting their Saturday's portion of alcohol while the huge lounge bar was filling, mostly with young people. Groups had formed at perhaps fifty tables. The majority comprised from three to five people, although a couple of tables had ten or more around them. The groups on the whole were closely segregated, with the girls and the young men stiffly ignoring each other. Only among the larger parties did the sexes mingle, except in the case of a few couples who seemed a little forlorn, isolated from the speculative tension over who would pair with whom before the day was done.

Peter Watts walked into the lounge with his hopes high, vaguely supposing that some attractive girl would turn and be stunned by his appearance, or just some girl. He stood for a moment in the doorway, unconsciously posing, and then the loneliness that he always forgot enveloped him. Nobody took any notice of him. Some other people were coming into the lounge behind him and he walked across to the bar, his hopes half rising when he passed a table at which five young girls were sitting, but sinking when they did not turn their heads.

'I'll have a beer, Mick,' he said, and Mick, who could serve beer faster than any man alive, had drawn the beer, taken Peter's money and given him change before Peter could formulate another sentence. Not that Mick would have answered anyway. He would often talk to a favoured customer, but these kids were just something you poured beer into, took money off, then threw out when they became too obstreperous. They'd keep on coming back and spending money no matter how he treated them, unless he banned them. It was difficult to be banned from the hotel unless you were given to practices that were financially damaging, like slashing the chairs.

Just a word from Mick would have made Peter feel like a man, but there was no word and he took his beer and sat at a vacant table trying to look as though he was waiting for someone. 'The Boys' that Peter had told his father he was going to meet didn't exist. He'd tried to join various groups since he'd left school. The few young men at his job spent all their spare daylight in the surf and Peter had once disastrously accompanied them. Because he was a bad swimmer he'd spent the day on the beach near the swimmers' girls. Near them, not with them. Because he wasn't one of the swimmers they'd ignored him and spent their own day lying on the hot sand, smoking, gazing at the hypnotic surf where the fledgling men were riding the waves. At night they'd lit a fire on the beach and drunk beer and smoked pot while Peter hung around the outskirts, watching, waiting in vain to be invited to join and finally going home, discarded by the little herd.

It was soon after that he'd bought his motor-cycle and somehow managed to give the impression to his parents and his workmates that he mixed with his own crowd. In fact he'd tried to scrape up an acquaintance with the various groups of bikies that frequented the hotel, but they'd contemptuously rebuffed him.

Once he even tried a church group in a desperate attempt to find some milieu in which to exist but that little herd, because of his long, beautiful hair and fanciful clothes, had rejected him quite as firmly as the others had.

So now he sat in the lounge bar, sipping at the beer he didn't like, looking around for someone to love.

John Verdon caught sight of Peter over the rim of his glass and slammed the glass down theatrically.

'Christ,' he said loudly: 'Look at that fucker, will you?'

Harris turned and saw Peter a few tables away, in his gorgeous shirt and long blond hair. He laughed, making that strange humourless sound that is intended as an insult to its object. Peter didn't hear. He was looking at a blonde, plump girl at the next table who, he thought, was naked under her see-through blouse. He couldn't see any brassière straps and he fancied he could distinguish the darker tones of her nipples as she leaned her breasts on the table the better to hear what her companion was saying. Soon he would go over to her and say 'let me buy you a drink', and she'd turn and smile up at him and quickly abandon her companions and come and sit with him. Then after a few drinks, because you always had to buy them a few drinks, he would suggest a ride on his motor-cycle and she would agree with a look that would let him know she knew exactly what he meant, and they would ride off into the countryside ...

The girl sat up straight and Peter could see that she was in fact wearing a brassière.

'Look at the fucker,' said Verdon again, and then finding his glass was empty and remembering that it was his turn to buy a round, stood up and walked over to the bar.

Peter was leaning back on his chair and as Verdon passed it he kicked at one of the legs so that Peter nearly fell off. Verdon gave a contemptuous grunt and walked on. It was too early in the day to bother about the little poofter. One of the barmen saw the incident and marked Verdon down as one likely to cause trouble later. The barman resolved to keep away from the trouble when it happened as he saw the muscles in Verdon's forearms.

Peter didn't look up as Verdon walked past him. He was used to actions like that. In a way he couldn't explain he didn't particularly mind. Several other people had noticed and were looking at Peter. He didn't mind that either.

Counsel for the Defence:

The publican was so pre-occupied with the affairs of the hotel that he was in no position accurately to observe and remember the early events of that day.

Counsel for the Prosecution:

The publican was a man who by nature and habit closely observed every minor detail of the workings of the hotel.

The Judge:

Both Counsel have thought it proper to bring detailed evidence of events in the hotel that day, and much of this you may well find irrelevant.

Mick made a quick survey of the hotel. Trade was building and he could feel it was going to be a big day. In the public bar he saw a new barman giving a full measure of whisky and made a note to talk to him later. Mick expected at least thirty, and preferably thirty-two, one ounce servings of spirits from a twenty-six ounce bottle. He personally instructed every bartender in the art of serving the nip quickly, tossing the whisky into the measure and from the measure into the glass in almost one movement, so that the measure was never quite full.

'The measure's wider at the top than it is at the bottom so even a fraction of an inch makes a big difference,' he would say. 'You've got to watch it, son. You've got to watch it. That's the way you make your wages. All pubs do it. You've got to, son, you've got to.'

The short measure principle applied even when selling inferior whisky from better brand bottles. It was literally a matter of principle with Mick. He was meticulously honest with the owner of the hotel and scrupulously passed on to him the benefits of short measuring and brand changing. It would have been as completely against Mick's code as a publican to cheat his owners as it would have been not to cheat his customer.

Mick moved on to the lounge bar. It was satisfyingly full. It would be completely crowded in half an hour's time when the band was due to start. Mick walked through the tiny dance floor space vaguely waving in response to many cries of 'How are you, Mick? When you gonna shout,

Mick? Come and have a drink, Mick,' because Mick, like so many quite self-contained men, was rather popular.

In the office Jenny was making up the room bookings.

'How's it going, love?' asked Mick.

'Just about full for tonight. Got a couple up m'sleeve.'

'Any of the usual's taken?'

'Not yet. But they'll be pretty busy today, looking at the crowd.'

The usuals were the six rooms that Mick kept reserved for casual use. Couples would hire them for the night, but only use them for an hour or two. Mick and Jenny had become adept at picking those who would not stay the night and consequently managed to let the six rooms several times each on a good night. Quite often they didn't even have to change the sheets – just make the bed up again. Once a drunk had accused Mick of running a brothel and Mick, quite unoffended, had explained that this was completely untrue. He would never let a room to a prostitute because a prostitute might well entertain several customers but the room would only produce one night's rental.

'Has the band arrived yet?'

'They're just getting out of their truck now.'

'Good. Tell them to start as soon as they can.' Mick engaged the band from four in the afternoon until ten at night on Saturdays, but he always tried to persuade them to start a little early because he felt he obtained better value that way. As soon as the band started the serving rate at the bar would increase because the dancers tended to finish their drinks quickly before standing up to dance, then order another one as soon as they'd finished. By keeping the periods of music short and frequent, Mick had found he could virtually dictate the drinking rate.

'Give Mol a feed if you get a chance,' said Mick, as he trotted off on his rounds, a vast bulk of dedication neatly weaving his way around the tables and side-stepping drinkers.

He popped into the men's toilets to see that all was well there and finding two youths urinating abjured them, 'Stand up close there, boys, stand up close, don't want other blokes walking in your piss.'

One of the cubicles was closed and Mick rattled the handle. 'All right in there?' he called, because occasionally a drunk passed out in a cubicle and kept it occupied longer than he ought.

An indistinguishable curse answered him, but the voice was strained and Mick's sensitive ear caught something wrong.

'All right in there?' he called again, peremptorily.

Again the strained reply, but this time ending in the un-mistakable sound of someone vomiting.

Mick took out a key and opened the door. A youth was leaning against the wall of the cubicle, his eyes streaming, fluid dripping from his mouth.

'Fuck off,' gasped the youth.

Mick glanced around the cubicle, looking for signs of any inaccuracy on the youth's part. He had been known to demand and obtain a cleaning fee from an offending customer in similar circumstances.

The youth began to retch again and Mick stood back. He didn't want any mess on the floor. The youth finished and leaned against the wall gasping. Mick studied him.

'You'd better go for a bit of a walk. You'll be right then.'

The youth wiped his sleeve across his face and nodded.

'You'll be right, mate,' Mick patted him on the shoulder as he left the lavatory.

Mick knew the boy would walk around the hotel, then come back in and start drinking once more. Eventually he would vomit again and this time he might not be so neat, but in the meantime he would have drunk another six or eight glasses of beer. The profit from that would more than cover any cleaning cost and with any luck Mick might be able to stick the boy with a cleaning charge anyway.

'You'll be right, mate,' said Mick again. 'Just go for a bit of a walk.'

Verdon came back to his table with another round of drinks. He'd forgotten about Peter now and his eyes were casting about for some bird. He had a very simple procedure with women. He would go around to all those that attracted him and say, 'Do you want a fuck?' Usually he was refused, but in the course of a day's drinking, and provided he put his question to enough girls, he often got what he wanted. What he wanted was a brutal brief encounter either in one of Mick's 'usuals' or in the bush between the hotel and the cliffs. He never bothered to undress or required his partner to undress because he didn't want his sexual activities to interfere too much with his drinking time. The alcohol in his bloodstream usually blunted what pleasure there was for him in such encounters. He mainly did it because he expected it of himself and he knew from experience that if he didn't have some sort of sexual release a few times a week he became uncomfortable. He invariably left the girl without a word and buttoned up his trousers as he made his way back to the bar. The girls didn't care much because they were usually too drunk to know what was happening anyway.

Quite often, if the object of his attention happened to be accompanied by a male, his direct question led immediately to a fight. But this was all right by Verdon, as much a part of the week-end activity as fornicating.

He stopped by a table at which five girls were sitting and leaned over a big bosomed brunette.

'Do you want a fuck?' he said.

The girl, who looked about fifteen and had a rather sweet expression, was drinking Coca Cola and Marsala through a straw.

She didn't even look up at Verdon.

'Fuck off,' she said.

Verdon shrugged and made his way back to his own table. Two other young men from the meatworks had joined Bob Harris who was telling some story that necessitated his holding both hands clasped above his head and bringing them down on the table rapidly several times as though clubbing something.

'I was just telling 'em,' said Harris, choking with laughter, 'I was just telling 'em, Johnny, about that steer this morning.

'Jesus, men,' he said to the others, 'you should have seen old Johnny here; he jumped straight into the pen with that old bugger and just about knocked his head off. Old Johnny here doesn't like it when they don't fall down quickly, do you, Johnny?

'But I tell you what, Johnny,' said Harris, turning solemn. 'Not many men would have done what you done. It's no joke to get into the pen with a steer like that, particularly not when his snout's smashed in. That makes 'em real vicious that does.'

'Well, what do you do?' said Verdon modestly. He didn't mind the reference to the bungled kill. It happened so infrequently that it didn't matter, and it happened less frequently to him than to the other hammer men.

'Well, I know what I bloody well would do,' said Vic Parson, who worked as a boner, 'I'd bloody well call for the gun I would. You wouldn't get me going into the pen with a bloody steer that was still kickin'.'

'Me either,' said Jim Marshall, who worked on the flaying floor.

The relationship between these two and Harris and Verdon was rather like the relationship between the conductor and the driver on a bus. They were in the same field and there was easy intercourse between them, but the killing men felt themselves to be, and were felt to be, possessed of superior skills and consequently higher status. Similarly there was a difference between Verdon who swung the hammer and Harris who cut the throats. This relationship was much like that between the flight captain and the co-pilot on an aircraft.

'I never called for the gun yet,' said Verdon. 'Calling for the gun' was the practice when a particularly difficult beast took too much killing and was dispatched with a rifle.

'You'd be about the only man on the job who hasn't,' said Harris.

'Yeah, well those fuckers don't really know how to kill.' Verdon was the youngest hammer man ever to work at the meatworks. He'd come down from the country at eighteen and got a job on the flaying floor. When he was nineteen a hammer man had fallen into the pen and broken his arm. Verdon had volunteered for the job.

'Ever killed?' asked the foreman.

'My fuckin' oath,' said Verdon. 'Killed all our own stuff at home.'

'With a hammer?'

'With a hammer, with an axe, any fuckin' thing you like. Give me a go, you'll see.'

The foreman hadn't been keen because the RSPCA inspectors were very meticulous and any stories of mangled beasts were likely to cause trouble; but it was a heavy killing day and there was no other hammer man available, so Verdon got his chance.

The foreman relaxed even before Verdon struck the first blow. He had walked on to the platform above the killing chute and tested the hammer with a few smooth professional swings. Then he nodded and the foreman let in the first beast.

Verdon grinned as the hammer swung and he felt for the first time in more than a year the groin pleasure of killing. He hit the beast squarely between the eyes and it went down as though its legs had vanished.

Verdon had been a hammer man ever since and had never lost the sense of pleasure he felt when the hammer went home.

'It's hard to explain,' he told his friends in the bar, 'but if you can really do that job you don't make many mistakes. I tell you,' his eyes slightly moist, 'I tell you it's great to make a clean kill. You feel the hammer going through the bone and somehow it does something in your guts – something runs straight up out of that hammer head and down your arms and into your guts. I'd reckon if you haven't got that you'll never make a good hammer man.'

Verdon drank another half glass of beer.

'And you can tell whether you've done it right because of the way the hammer goes in. Even if you're an inch or two out from that one spot it feels different. But if you're on that spot the hammer goes in and that's when you get this real thrill. Jesus fuckin' Christ it's great.'

He took another drink and added. 'Something to do with doing the job right, I suppose.'

His companions, respectful before this poetic fancy, nodded solemnly.

'Come on, Bob. Your shout,' said Verdon.

Counsel for the Defence:

Peter Watts came to the hotel to pick up a girl. He was in a state of mind, on his own admission, which could well have led him to the deed which would justify John Verdon's actions. Whether he perpetrated that deed or not is for you to decide. But if you decide that he did, then John Verdon is certainly innocent.

Counsel for the Prosecution:

On the evidence it is obvious that Peter Watts came to the
hotel with nothing in mind other than a day of relaxation.
It is not unusual for youths to be interested in meeting girls.

The Judge:

Bear in mind that you are making a judgement of fact, not of morals.

Peter Watts had drunk three glasses of beer now and was wishing the band would start. When there was dancing you could just get in the crowd and dance because nobody touched each other and it was difficult to tell whether you were with anybody or not. You just stood there and shook your body and your arms and legs and moved your feet if you wanted to, and often you could bump into a girl and grab her a bit as though you were trying to stop her falling over. Or when there were girls dancing together you could sort of dance near them and get the feeling that you were dancing with them. Except that often they woke up to what you were doing and turned their backs on you. Perhaps they wouldn't turn their backs today, now he had his new shirt. But the shirt hadn't done him much good so far. A few men had made remarks about him, loudly and pointedly, but that often happened.

The band was setting up now. Three men, organ, drum and guitar and a tall blonde girl with long hair. Good-looking girl, nice pair of tits Peter told himself maturely; but a bit old for him.

That brunette over there had a beaut pair, Peter thought; she'd obviously knocked back the silly bugger who tried to turn his chair over. Maybe she was waiting for him. She would have had to notice him because he was between her and the band and she kept looking at the band. He wondered should he smile at her? Better just go right up to her and ask her to dance. Should he go now and ask? No, better wait until the band started. She was only a kid. One of the few girls in the bar a great deal younger than himself. Probably he'd seem something of a man to her. That's probably why she knocked the other bloke back. Too old for her.

The band was tuning up now. As soon as they started he'd go and ask the girl. He would all right. He'd just go up to her and say, 'How about a dance' and she, well she was young, she might look around at her friends and give a bit of a giggle, but then she'd get up and walk over to the floor. Perhaps he'd take her hand then and let it go when they were on the dance floor. Then they'd stand next to each other and they'd dance. She wouldn't be wearing a brassière and her tits would flop up and down as she danced and he'd be standing real close. Then when the dance finished she'd come back to his table and they'd have a drink. Then they'd have another dance and after that he'd tell her that he had a motor-bike. That'd impress a young kid like that. And she'd more or less ask him to take her for a ride. They'd go for a ride and he'd burn along some back road to frighten her a bit and she'd hang on tight so that her tits squashed up against his back. Then after a while they'd stop . . .

The band started. A blaring chord on the organ, a double thud on the drums, then, with the deep guitar backing slow, throbbing and rhythmic, the contralto of the girl singer, prophetically:

There is a house in New Orleans,
It's called the Rising Sun.
It's been the ruin of many a poor boy,
And of these I am one.

Immediately the small dance area filled. Perhaps a hundred dancers took the floor in a matter of seconds and stood in a tight-packed group making motions with their bodies in time to the music. Somehow or other the sex-segregated groups at the tables had mingled on the dance floor without a word being said, and perhaps three quarters of the dancers were paired off. The other quarter were girls, dancing together or alone. The distinction between being together or alone wasn't great because the dancers tended to stay in one place and merely directed the movements of their bodies in the general direction of their partners. The brunette whom Peter had been admiring had gone on to the floor with her table companions within seconds of the music starting. She was dancing in a group of three girls, her eyes closed, her body writhing to the rhythm of the song.

Peter finished his beer and walked on to the dance floor, standing as near as he could to the brunette. In fact he was a few feet to the side of her, but he stood and rolled his hips and shoulders and stared at the profile of the girl in the hope that it might appear that he was with her. Anybody watching would have seen only a pimply youth, with gaping mouth, staring at a girl who was dancing in a world of her own.

What neither Peter nor the girl realized was that she was so drunk that she had no idea where she was or what she was doing. Some deep impulse of her glands had sent her on to the floor when the music started, but her mind was rolling down a black and sliding tide that is not uncommon in fifteen-year-old girls who have been drinking steadily for five hours without having eaten anything since the night before.

Peter edged a little closer. He wanted to get in front of her so that she would notice him. It was very clear to him now that she wasn't wearing a brassière and her youthful breasts, large and soft, rose and fell with the rhythm of the song. Peter could see the nipple of her right breast, sliding up and down under the transparent flimsy blouse.

He moved a little closer, then someone bumped into him and he stumbled, almost fell over, and found himself face to face with the girl, his body almost touching hers.

The girl had her eyes shut and had no idea that Peter was there, but Peter found himself with the girl's breasts sliding up and down, almost touching his new shirt. He stood where he was and began to let his body follow the rhythm again. Anybody looking at them now would have thought they were partners.

Verdon and Harris's friends deserted them for the dance floor. Verdon and Harris, who never danced, looked disdainfully at the crowd wondering with some justification at the inanity of their contemporaries.

'Hey,' said Verdon suddenly. 'Look at that little poofter fucker dancing with the bird with the big boobs. The cheeky little shit.'

'It's probably his sister,' said Harris. 'That's about the only sort of fucking a shit like that would do.'

Verdon stared at Peter. That girl was the one he'd spoken to. She'd knocked him back. And there she was dancing with a little poofter. She knocked back him, John Verdon, and was dancing with a poofter.

'A man oughta cut that bastard's balls off and shove 'em down his throat,' he said by way of light conversation to his companion.

'He probably hasn't got any,' said Harris.

But, unconsoled, Verdon continued to stare at Peter Watts, apparently ecstatically dancing within inches of the big boobs which Verdon had coveted, or which at any rate had motivated his social impulse.

There was a fight on the verandah at the rear of the hotel. Two young men, blond, long-haired, stripped to the waist, were locked in a tangle of limbs on the concrete floor. The two girls who were with them, both rather drunk, wandered down to the other end of the verandah holding their beer glasses. They didn't mind the fighting, but they didn't want to get in the way of an accidental blow.

The two men each had handfuls of the other's hair and were trying to drive their knees into each other's bodies. Mostly their knees collided, but occasionally a blow would go home. Neither seemed to feel the pain of the blows nor the pulling at his hair, perhaps because they were too anaesthetized with alcohol, but their expressions were ferocious and the kicking and gouging seemed directed towards serious mutilation.

One jerked his head back suddenly and the other's hands came away clutching locks of hair. Still with the hair in his hands he drove his right fist at the other man's throat and felt the larynx collapse as the blow went home.

The injured man fell backwards and went to his knees. His protagonist tried to kick him in the back of the head, but missed. The injured man stood up again, but went reeling backwards. The two girls intervened before the victor could follow up his advantage, but the injured man, gasping and whooping, fell through the doorway leading from the verandah to the public bar.

Inside he stood up again and tried to speak, but his throat was so full of blood that he was almost drowning.

Mick happened to be in the public bar at the time. Looking up to see a customer coughing blood on the floor, he acted promptly. He vaulted over the bar, not an inconsiderable feat for a man of his size, trotted across to the injured man, picking him up by the shoulders and pushed him out of the door on to the verandah.

'You'd better look after your mate,' he said to the two girls and the other man, who, aware now that the matter had turned serious, were gaping anxiously at the blood dribbling out of their companion's mouth.

'We'd better ring a doctor,' said one of the girls.

'You do that, girlie,' said Mick. 'You'll find a public 'phone down the road.'

'Can't I ring from the pub?' said the girl.

'No. It's got nothing to do with the pub. I don't know what's happened. Nobody here knows what's happened. You go and ring a doctor or take your boyfriend down to the hospital. Right. Got that? Now push off and don't cause trouble.'

The injured man now had almost lost consciousness and was lying on the concrete floor of the verandah with the blood leaking from his mouth in a steady pulsating flow.

'Christ, mate, he's crook,' said one of the girls.

'Yes, well you take him to the hospital,' said Mick, retreating into the public bar.

When the two girls tried to follow him, begging to be allowed to use the telephone, he pushed them back, then closed and bolted the doors.

Jenny, who had observed the incident, said, 'That boy doesn't seem too good, Mick.'

'He'll be all right,' said Mick. 'Just got to keep them off the premises though, we don't want any trouble.'

'No. Of course not, dear. But he doesn't seem to be able to stand up.'

'Nor would you if you'd drunk twenty or thirty schooners,' said Mick, who seldom drank himself, virtuously. 'Drunken young bastard.'

The fact that Mick had personally served the young man with most of the twenty or thirty schooners he had drunk that day did not weigh heavily with him.

The two girls and their companion finally dragged the injured man into a car and drove him ten miles to the casualty ward of the district hospital. He survived and was out of hospital in a week.

When the music ended Peter was still facing the brunette. The floor emptied quickly, but the girl stood there, her eyes still closed, her body still convulsively swaying to the re-membered rhythm. Peter stayed in front of her, trying to gain courage to speak and he was astonished when she simply held out her hand. He took it wonderingly and stood there for some seconds looking at it. He had no way of knowing that the girl was literally unconscious on her feet.

Still unable to find anything to say and reluctant to release her hand, Peter turned and led the girl to his table. He was amazed that she went with him and while he couldn't make sense of the fact that she just stood by the chair he offered her, solved the problem by gallantly push-ing it against the backs of her knees. She subsided into the chair and finally opened her eyes.

'What'll ... what'll you drink?' croaked Peter, unable to believe that he was actually saying this to a real live girl.

The girl grinned and nodded and Peter didn't like to take the matter further, so he just went over to the bar and ordered beer for himself and a double Scotch and Coca Cola for the girl. He had observed that most girls liked their drinks mixed with Coca Cola and he had ordered the double Scotch on the basis of a quite accurate instinct that the more alcohol he poured into her the better it would be for his purposes.

The girl's companions, seeing her 'fixed up' had grinned to each other then forgotten her, intent now on seeing what their own fate would be.

Peter brought back the Scotch and the beer to the table and placed the Scotch near the girl's hand.

'I'm Peter Watts,' he said tentatively.

The girl nodded amiably and finding the glass at her hand picked it up and drained it because she was vaguely aware that she was terribly thirsty.

Peter was gratified, secure in the knowledge that he'd been paid yesterday and had plenty of money in his pockets.

'Would you like another one?' he said.

The girl didn't answer and Peter, who felt he was beginning to understand the form of communication, went to buy her another double whisky.

While he was at the bar the local police sergeant, a tall, heavily-built, grey-haired man, embodying authority in his uniform came into the bar to 'have a look around'.

Mick hurried to meet him. The police sergeant was one of the few people who were always sure of obtaining Mick's immediate attention. The sergeant was so well paid to ignore any irregularities he found in the hotel that Mick need never have spoken a friendly word to him, but Mick believed in following the form of the thing.

'Have a drink, sergeant,' said Mick, knowing well what the answer would be.

'Now while I'm on duty, Mick,' said the sergeant, loudly. Then he turned and surveyed the lounge bar. Peter happened to be alongside him and the sergeant looked down distastefully at his bare feet.

'No one under age here, Mick?' asked the sergeant, looking pointedly at Peter.

'No, sergeant. Nobody ever under age in my pub. This fellow here's about the youngest on the premises,' said Mick, gesturing at Peter. 'How old are you, son? You're over eighteen aren't you?'

'Yeah,' said Peter.

'Course you are. Nobody here under eighteen, sergeant.'

It was a pantomime largely for the benefit of any interfering citizen who might well have felt prompted to report the activities of the hotel to the Licensing Board.

The sergeant looked around the lounge again, his gaze falling on the girl at Peter's table. He had in fact met her. She went to school with his own fifteen-year-old daughter. But he did not recognize her out-of-school uniform. He would not have spoken to her anyway. He was wary of direct questions to drinkers ever since he'd asked a drunken girl in the lounge bar whether or not she was eighteen.

'I will be in a couple of years, Mister,' she had replied.

For the sake of form Mick had been obliged to eject a good paying customer, and that did not accord with the spirit of the agreement between Mick and the police sergeant.

'No trouble, Mick?' said the sergeant.

'None at all, sergeant. Never any trouble in my pub. You know that,' said Mick, not even glancing out on to the verandah where a yardsman was sluicing a bucket of water over the pools of blood.

Peter went back to his girl and gave her the whisky. She drained that as nonchalantly as the first. Peter himself had now drunk five glasses of beer and was feeling unusually self-confident. The girl's left hand was on the table and Peter put his own hand over it. The girl didn't take it away so Peter assumed he was sitting in a bar holding the hand of a girl whom shortly he would take for a ride on his motor-bike.

Verdon was aware of an increasing sense of irritation. It was getting late on Saturday afternoon and he hadn't fornicated. His normal week-end activities involved two episodes on Saturday and one on Sunday because he was usually feeling a bit off on Sunday mornings.

There were considerable and exotic variations in his sexual programme but he was never quite sure what they were because, as often as not, he couldn't remember what he'd done over the week-end. However, two on Saturday and one on Sunday was a good basic programme to go by, he felt.

By now he and his mate had lapsed into a solemn silence apart from their raucous belching. They sat in their chairs staring at every female form they could see with something of the solid patience of a bull casting around for a cow in heat. Verdon had put his simplistic proposition to several girls, but he had had no luck so far. He wasn't discouraged. That would have been too complex an emotion for him, but he was irritated.

He could see Peter and the brunette quite clearly and the contact of their hands inflamed his irritation. The bitch was obviously willing to screw and yet she had knocked him back. That little poofter perving on her hand ought to have his balls kicked in. Playing hands was about all he'd be good for. Why didn't he let the girls alone anyway and stick with his own kind?

Verdon had considered going and asking the brunette again on the grounds that there had obviously been some misunderstanding on her part the first time, but one of his points of pride was that he never asked a girl twice.

The band started again, a great blurt of sound that overwhelmed the high babble of voices in the bar, that overwhelmed thought and feeling and any form of human communication other than words shouted directly into the ear.

Verdon saw Peter lead the brunette to the dance area again. He spat copiously on to the carpeted floor. He could see the brunette's breasts moving as she danced, and while he was usually not so interested in the delicacies of sexual activity as to be concerned with secondary manifestations, his present state of comparative celibacy made him unusually sensitive. He wasn't aware of a sense of profound sexual jealousy; only that he was enveloped in a vicious rage, directed towards Peter.

'I think I'll go and break that poofter's spine,' he said to Harris, who nodded solemnly, as though that were the most natural thing in the world to do.

Verdon had actually lurched to his feet when he was diverted. Two girls had come into the bar. Both were wearing skirts which was unusual in that company, and top pieces which did little to conceal their curving, luscious breasts.

They stopped in the doorway, peered interestedly around the lounge, then immediately went to the dance floor and began dancing together.

Verdon walked straight across to the nearest girl and put his usual question to her.

They were only a couple of feet from the band amplifiers and the girl didn't hear, but she knew Verdon was speaking to her and she smiled and shrugged her shoulders.

Verdon put his mouth against her ear and bellowed his five word question.

The girl caught it this time and bellowed back to Verdon, 'Five bucks.'

Verdon misunderstood, confused by the sound level and the rhyming qualities involved in the conversation.

'I should be able to manage that,' he bellowed, thinking the bitch would be lucky to get more than one bang out of him; he didn't like using the same girl twice unless he had to.

He grabbed the girl by the arm and they walked off the dance floor, and out of the lounge bar.

'Johnny's right,' thought Harris, and determined that he too must soon make some arrangement. 'Otherwise I'll be too pissed,' he added wisely to himself.

Verdon wondered whether to take the girl down to the beach but decided against it on the grounds that too much time would be consumed. He presented himself at the office of the hotel and said to Jenny: 'Want a room for the night.'

Jenny sized them up as classic candidates for the 'usuals' and said, 'Ten dollars bed and breakfast.'

Verdon almost said he didn't want any bloody breakfast, but he had been through this before and dimly that there were norms to be observed. He handed over the ten dollars, took the key to the room and clumped up the stairs with the girl following.

Verdon opened the door of the room and left the girl to shut it. By the time she'd managed this, and discreetly pushed the bolt in, he had his trousers open. He grabbed her by the shoulders and pushed her towards the bed.

'Easy, mate, easy,' said the girl.

'Easy be fucked,' said Verdon, thrusting her down on her back and dragging her skirt up.

She was conveniently wearing no underclothing so Verdon was saved his normal expenditure of energy in ripping away any obstacle to his intentions.

'Hey easy, mate,' squealed the girl, as Verdon speared at her. She didn't mind the haste because the shorter the job the greater her earning capacity, but she didn't want her tools of trade damaged.

Verdon had a little trouble finding his way but the girl, accepting the inevitable, guided him, and after half a dozen violent thrusts he achieved a third of his week-end quota.

He pulled away, rolled off the bed and began walking to the door, pulling up the zip fastener on his fly as he went.

'Hold it,' said the girl sharply, sitting up and hygienically dabbing at her thighs with the bed quilt.

Verdon half turned but kept walking.

'Hold it,' cried the girl again. 'Five bucks, matie.'

Astounded, Verdon stopped and turned.

'What?' he said.

'Five bucks. I told you it'd cost you five bucks.'

Verdon did not advert to the mistake that had been made. All he knew was that this bloody slut was asking him for money. He had never paid for it in his life.

The girl pulled her skirt down and stood up.

'Come on, chiseller,' she said. 'Five bucks.'

Had he been given to argument, Verdon would have told the girl that the fact that he had paid ten dollars for the hotel room made her request even more outrageously unjust than it appeared on the surface, and in any case the notion was fantastic.

So fantastic that he gave a grunting laugh as he made the last pull on his zip fastener. The fastener caught in his pubic hair and gave him a moment of acute pain. He winced and pulled the fastener down again.

The girl laughed. Verdon took a swipe at her and missed, and then, because she wasn't worth the trouble, turned and went. She tried to stop him leaving the room, but he pushed her back and she sat down heavily.

'You'll pay before the day's out, you bastard,' called the girl to his retreating back. Then she adjusted her clothing and went back into the lounge bar. It was all in the day's work really and she did have an actual hope of obtaining her just payment.

Jenny, pattering upstairs to inspect the room after the couple had gone past the office, was delighted to find that she had only to smooth down the rumpled bed quilt. The key to the room was still in the door. The next occupant was in possession within half an hour.

When Verdon rejoined his friends, Harris said: 'Your fly's open, Johnny.'

Verdon grunted and carefully pulled up the zip fastener, then reached for the first of the two beers which Harris had conscientiously left for him as he had drunk his own.

When the music stopped, Peter took the brunette's hand and led her back to the table. She still hadn't spoken a word to him and Peter didn't mind because it made life much easier for him. In some way the girl seemed to have given herself into his hands.

'Would you like another drink?' he said when they sat down. The girl sat there, her arms on the table, her eyes unfocused, staring blankly beyond Peter's head.

Peter wondered about buying another drink. He didn't want any more himself, not yet anyway.

The girl began to grin foolishly, lost in some dream of her own. Peter took it as a sign of affection.

'I've got a motor-bike,' he said.

The girl kept grinning.

'Would you like a ride?' said Peter. Strangely enough it was all going much as he had imagined it would, except that the girl wasn't saying anything.

She still said nothing, and Peter, who now intuitively knew that she would do whatever he led her to do, stood up and took her hand to raise her out of the chair.

Obediently she stood up, vaguely aware that there was no music and that this was not the time to be standing up, but much too far gone to do anything about it.

Still holding her hand, Peter led her out through the front door of the hotel and around to the parking area where he'd left his motor-cycle. His helmet was locked to the handle-bars and as he undid the lock he wondered whether to offer the helmet to the girl.

'Would you like the helmet?' he said, holding it out to her.

Still just the glassy grin.

Gently Peter put the helmet on her head. Because she had thick hair it wasn't a bad fit. He tied the strap under her chin and let down the eyeshield. In her blouse and jeans the girl was transformed into one of the extraterrestrial-looking neuters that ride motor-cycles; neuter if seen from the rear anyway. Peter regretted that he'd put the helmet on because she didn't seem so much like a girl, but it didn't matter because he'd take it off again when they stopped after they'd had their ride.

Peter straddled his motor-cycle and started the engine.

'Hop on and put your arms around me,' he said, feeling the words thick in his throat.

The girl stood where she was, anonymous and unresponsive under the dark eye-shield.

'Hop on,' shouted Peter. 'Just hop on behind me.'

But she still stood there.

Puzzled, but accepting the phenomenon as part of a world with which he was unfamiliar, Peter reached out and took her by the arm. Placidly she allowed herself to be drawn close to the machine.

'Just put your leg over the seat,' said Peter. But no words were getting through to the girl.

Peter leaned down and grasped at the girl's jeans, trying to lift her leg over the pillion, excited at the feel of the plump flesh beneath the coarse material. The girl raised her leg and would have fallen over had Peter not still had hold of her hand. He gave a jerk and got her leg across the pillion seat, but she was still leaning too far to one side.

Anyway he realized she was facing the wrong way.

Peter, his confidence increasing with the total absence of any resistance from the girl, got off the bike, hitched the girl's leg over off the pillion, turned her round, hitched her leg back over the pillion and found he had her more or less in the right position.

He also found that as he was holding her his right hand was encountering the side of her right breast. He'd never felt a girl's breast before and he stood there, holding her, the motor still running, breathing in the exhaust fumes, consumed with the wonder of it. Then in a flurry of excitement he climbed on to the bike himself, still holding her, and guided her arms around his waist.

She slumped forward against him and he could feel, just as he had imagined it, her plump breasts squashed against his back. An edge of the helmet was grinding into his shoulder where her head had flopped but he ignored that.

'Hold on,' he called, and feeling she probably wasn't as securely seated as she ought to have been, he drove quite slowly out of the car park and on to the road. By the side of the hotel a dirt road ran from the highway down to the beach and Peter turned on to this.

He must have driven a full fifty yards before the girl fell off. She rolled backwards off the motor-cycle.

Peter stopped, dropped the motor-cycle on its side and ran back to her. She was sitting up in the dust giggling. At least Peter thought she was giggling. He couldn't tell because she still had the helmet on. He helped her up.

'You've got to hang on,' he said.

No reply.

A little helplessly, Peter said: 'Well look, would you sooner go for a walk?'

The giggling sounds from under the helmet.

'All right, just a minute.'

Peter went back, righted his motor-cycle and parked it by the side of the road.

'We'll go for a walk down to the beach,' he said. 'You'd better take that helmet off.' He didn't even expect answers now and he tried to undo the straps around her neck. But her hands came up and grabbed his and her head was shaking. Peter took this to mean that she wanted to keep the helmet on. He didn't understand, but in view of what he hoped to gain from her company he wasn't disposed to argue.

'Come on then.' He took her hand and led her off the road to a path leading down to the beach.

Peter found a sandy alcove among some bushes close to the water. It was a cool day so there weren't many people on the beach, not that privacy was the greatest of Peter's concerns, but he didn't want anybody interfering. If he stood up in the little grove he could see over the bushes to the surf and up the slope to the hotel a few hundred yards away. He could hear quite clearly the blare of the band, but so could everybody else within a radius of a mile. The fact that even down here the sound of the surf was lost in the noise of the band was not remarkable to Peter, any more than was the great brown stain spreading out into the sea from the hotel's sewer outlet in front of him. Pouring untreated sewage into the sea was a natural economy for the hotel and the local council wasn't disposed to be harsh in the matter. Other detritus from the hotel, beer cans, pie crusts, paper, littered the beach and Peter's sandy grove, but these were as much part of his environment as the trees and shrubs that surrounded him, more in fact.

He sat down and drew the girl down beside him.

She crossed her legs, dropped her hands on her lap and let her head sag. Peter thought she was shy. Probably that was why she kept the helmet on.

The girl had passed out cold and when Peter leaned forward to touch her shoulder she rolled over backwards and lay flat with her arms outspread and her legs still crossed.

Tentatively Peter ran his hand down her arm. No response. He touched her shoulder. She didn't stir. As if by accident he let his hand rest on her stomach and felt the delicious warmth under the blouse.

Fearfully he undid the bottom button of her blouse, then the second, the third, and soon all the glory of her soft young breasts was revealed to him, spreading gentle curves of white and pink flesh. Gently, trembling, he took her breasts in both hands.

He squeezed and kneaded and stroked and took his fill of the breasts, a little disappointed that he evoked no response in her, but willing to take things as they came.

Some improbable sense of delicacy prevented him making another attempt to take off the helmet. He supposed she wanted to keep it on, and that was all right by him.

He had a lot of trouble with her jeans. They were tight and her legs were crossed. He managed to uncross her legs, but then made the mistake of trying to roll the jeans down from her hips. He became terribly excited at the sight of her pink underwear and jerked and dragged at the jeans until they ended in an impossible tangle around her knees.

Panting, he stopped to consider, then pulled the jeans up again and began dragging them off by the ends of the legs.

The jeans conquered, the underwear presented no difficulties and Peter soon found himself possessed of the vision of a totally naked young girl, her arms flung wide, her breasts presented to him, her legs apart, flat on her back.

The slight incongruity of the helmet hiding her face did not particularly upset him.

Quickly he began to drag off his own clothes.

Counsel for the Defence:

If Peter Watts raped, or attempted to rape the girl, then John Verdon's later act was justifiable.

Counsel for the Prosecution:

The only evidence you have on the question of rape comes from Verdon and Watts. Watts says Verdon committed the rape, Verdon says Watts committed the rape. That is all that has been said. The girl herself had no memory of the events, and all that later medical evidence showed was that intercourse had taken place. She had not been assaulted in any way.

The Judge:

You may well question the reliability of evidence on the matter of rape on the grounds that all relevant evidence comes from persons who on their own admission were substantially affected by alcohol. And while on this point, it must be remembered that the fact that a person is drunk is in no way a defence against any charge.

There was a certain ritual in the way the prostitute's protector approached Verdon. He had two friends with him and they were all big men a few years older than the meatworkers, heavily muscled, a little slow moving but very strong. All three men were quite sober.

They walked deliberately up to Verdon's table and stood looking down at him.

'Hey, mate,' said the protector. 'I'd like five bucks off you.'

The meatworkers looked up in silence. They weren't sure what this was about, but even through their beer-drenched senses, they smelt violence. That was all right, it was part of the week-end, but there was a certain form to be gone through first.

The protector didn't want a fight in the hotel. He knew that this was likely to cause damage and lead to his being banned. But he'd done this many times and he knew exactly how to set the scene as he wanted it.

Verdon, a bull smelling a challenger, sat up straighter, 'What's wrong with you?'

The protector said: 'I want five bucks off you. Come on, mate, give.'

'What's wrong with you?'

Patiently the protector said: 'You got your end in and now you've got to pay. Come on.'

'How would you like a kick in the balls?'

'Mate, I can take you apart and chop you up into shit in ten seconds, and I will unless you hand over five bucks.'

Verdon was incapable of fear even when he was sober and now he spat at the big man's feet.

'Why don't you fuck off?'

'All right, mate, how about coming down to the beach?'

Verdon had more or less expected to be hit where he was and he'd contemptuously waited for the other man to throw the first blow. Now he realized that this was a more formal challenge. It wasn't to be an all-in brawl between him and his mate and these other three men, it was to be a personal contest between him and this one man. Which suited him just as well.

He stood up suddenly so that his chair fell over, drawing a quick look from Mick, who immediately realized what was happening and reached for the ebony stick under the counter.

But he relaxed when Verdon went barging through the dancers followed by his mate Harris and more slowly by the other three men. This was the sort of brawl Mick approved of; it was going to happen off the premises.

Outside the hotel Verdon plunged off down the slope towards the beach. He'd done this in various forms often enough before and he headed towards a spot which, for reasons known only to himself if reasons there were, he considered suitable for such encounters. Harris stayed close beside him and the other three followed.

Mick watched them until they were out of sight. He didn't want any bastard running back to the hotel with his guts hanging out, but he was fairly confident because he'd seen the three big men in action before and their victims were seldom in a position to move anywhere, much less back to the hotel.

'Yes, son, what'll you have?' he said to the youth who had ranged up to the bar in front of him.

'Middy of rum, Mick,' said the youth.

Mick glanced at the clock. It was unusual to get a request such as this so early in the day. There was a local tradition among his younger customers that the last drink of the day should be a ten ounce glass of neat spirits.

'You going home early are you, Charley?' said Mick, who recognized the youth as the son of one of the regular local customers.

'Going to a dance, Mick,' said the youth, slurring badly, swaying on his feet. He'd been drinking beer steadily since midday and what remained of his brain was swimming in alcohol.

It never occurred to Mick not to give the boy his drink. Ten ounces of rum sold over the bar cost four dollars. The boy could have gone round to the bottle department and bought a thirteen ounce bottle of substantially better rum for less money, but that wasn't quite the point. The point was that you stood in front of your fellows and poured ten ounces of neat spirit down your throat. It was a custom Mick encouraged. Even with fair measure the profit on ten ounces was high, but Mick usually managed to get away with only nine ounces in the glass and he only sold cheap spirits in the lounge bar on Saturdays so he probably gained as much as three dollars profit on each glass.

Sometimes the boys ordered ten ounces of mixed spirits; whisky, vodka, rum and gin, and Mick made an even higher profit out of this. The effect on the drinkers was usually marked by a violent fit of vomiting, but most of them managed to remain on their feet until they reached their car.

Mick gave the boy his rum and took his four dollars.

'Thanks, Mick,' said the boy, 'have one yourself,' and dropped another forty cents on the bar.

'Thanks-mate-have-one-with-you-next-time,' recited Mick, scooping up the forty cents and putting it in his personal jar. This was one of the sources of income which, quite legitimately, he did not share with the owner of the hotel.

The boy weaved back to his table where three girls were staring blankly at four youths, waiting for the music to start again.

'Well, I'll be seeing you,' said the youth, standing where all could see that he was drinking a full glass of rum.

They stared at him dully and he did his best to drink the rum straight down. But it was too much for him, even in his anaesthetized state. He gasped for breath and had to stop several times. In the end he found he had to sit down and, in all, it took him almost ten minutes to absorb the rum. His companions meanwhile had gone back to the dance floor.

The youth dragged himself to his feet, scarcely aware of where he was, the alcohol in his bloodstream very nearly at the lethal point. Because of his familiarity with the route he found his way out of the hotel and even to his car in the parking lot. He had a lot of trouble getting the key into its slot, but once he had the motor going his body came under the control of the twentieth-century instinct which enables a man who can hardly stand to drive a car.

Unfortunately the instinct didn't help his vision much and he hadn't gone half a mile down the highway before he was driving at ninety miles an hour.

He ran under the rear of a semi-trailer and the tray tore his skull off just above his nose.

His alcohol-steeped brains were spread from one end of his car to the other.

Mick heard about the accident next day and wondered whether he should send some flowers to the funeral as he knew the boy's father vaguely. He decided not to because it might look as though he thought the hotel was involved in some way.

The youth died just as the realization struck Peter that seduction was not simple for the inexperienced. It was even less simple when one of the parties was paralytically drunk.

He was completely stripped himself, his clothes strewn with the girl's among the beer cans and rubbish of the little grove. The girl hadn't moved for the last ten minutes but Peter in his enthusiasm had managed to scatter a considerable amount of sand over both their bodies. Despite the slightly cool day, Peter was sweating and he found the sand clung to his skin.

A little to his surprise he discovered himself quite technically capable of what he proposed to do, but he was finding the mechanics utterly baffling. With the girl flattened on the sand there seemed to be no way he could begin the act, much less complete it.

Vaguely feeling that she could be helping, he tried a couple of times to stir her into action by rubbing her thighs, but she remained quite inert.

He thought of taking off the helmet but as his sense of inability increased he became grateful for the anonymity of the dark shield over the girl's face. Had she been looking at him as he fumbled and probed at her body, his resolution might well have collapsed.

The tremendous stimulus he felt when he'd first uncovered the girl's body had died away and now all he felt was a certain desperation, an almost academic desire to actually complete what he'd started.

And after a little while, to his horror, even his technical capacity drained away.

He squatted back on his haunches between the girl's parted legs and miserably wondered what to do next.

Verdon knew only one way of fighting – to go in and strike, kick and gouge until the other man was unconscious. Even sober he had a high threshold of pain and he'd found in many fights that in a simple exchange of punishment he could almost always outlast the other man.

Now, on a flat area of gravel in a car park near the beach, he stood for a moment contemplating his opponent. The other man was big and confident, but Verdon did not recognize this, nor would have cared if he had. What awareness he had only extended to the audience of Harris and his opponent's supporters. He would be justified in their eyes and his own in reducing the other man to a bloody mess. He didn't have any doubts about his ability to do this any more than he doubted his ability to dispatch a line of a hundred steers with few more than a hundred blows of the hammer.

When he began to break some part of the other man's body, his nose, his eyes, his limbs, he would feel a deeply sensuous gratification but this was not an incentive with him. He never thought about that until it had happened.

'Why don't you just hand over the five bucks and save yourself a lot of trouble?'

The contemptuous, provoking words produced the desired result on Verdon. He rushed at the other man, his arms flailing, knees kicking high, head down, intent on violent contact in any form.

A second later he was lying on his back on the gravel feeling as though somebody had hit him on the forehead with a club.

His opponent was grinning at his split knuckles. He'd meant to flatten Verdon's nose, but the blow had landed high. Never mind, he'd have plenty of chances.

Verdon scrambled to his feet and ran in again, this time to take a blow fair in the mouth. His teeth went through his bottom lip and as his hand went up to the mangled flesh a fist hit him in the eye and he felt something burst. He went backwards, half blinded, and he could feel blows thudding into his body, his face. He tried to cover up and kick but he couldn't see and he felt the fists pounding into the side of his head, his ear, his jaw and, for the first time, pain, agonizing enough to sear through the blanket of alcohol as knuckles smashed against his right kidney.

Harris looked dully on as Verdon scrabbled on the gravel, one hand pressed to his back the other trying to untangle his shattered lip from his teeth. Harris had enough sense of self-preservation not to interfere and in any case he'd seen old Johnny down before and still come back to win. If he'd been given to self-analysis he would have acknowledged that he hadn't seen old Johnny quite as down as this before.

Verdon rolled across the gravel, trying to avoid the boots he imagined would thud into his body. But there were no boots. His opponent was quite content to let him stand up and be knocked down again.

'Five bucks, mate.'

Verdon rose to a half crouch and flung himself at the other man's knees. One of the knees rose sharply and crushed his nose and he went over backwards with a choking howl.

His legs were spread apart, doubled under him, and the other man went in and gave him a sharp kick in the testicles, more in the way of poetic justice than with the intention of adding greatly to the damage.

Verdon convulsed on the ground, his hands flailing between the points of agony on his tortured flesh.

'Five bucks, mate,' and again in response to the taunting words Verdon tried to fling himself at the other man's legs. But he fell on his face before he could reach him and tore the skin off his cheek on the gravel.

The other man moved towards him, but Harris intervened.

'Hang on,' he said thickly, shaking his head as the other man's friends moved in anticipating trouble. 'Hang on, that's enough.' He dredged in his pocked and pulled out five dollars.

'Here y'are,' he said. 'That's enough.'

Verdon, squirming on the ground, heard.

'Fuck him. Don't pay the fucker.'

The other man grinned and took the five dollars.

'It's the fucker who pays, mate,' he said, and he turned and walked back towards the hotel.

'She's still working the pub if you're interested,' he called back. 'Just remember the price is five bucks.'

His companions laughed as they joined him and together they presented three broad backs to the meatworkers.

With the solicitude of a drunk Harris helped Verdon to his feet and dragged him over to a nearby tap to clear away the blood. Had Verdon been seriously hurt Harris's ministrations would probably have killed him, but he wasn't and Harris managed to clean him up after a fashion. Then, soaked with water and blood, his mouth gashed and still bleeding, one eye closed, the cartilage in his nose seriously misshapen, the flesh on his face raw and seeping fluid, Verdon said : 'Let's get a fuckin' drink.'

They started to walk back to the hotel, unafraid of further trouble with the prostitute's protectors, because that was all over now. It was as though two dogs had fought a bloody battle for supremacy and, once the victor was established, both realized there was no need for further fighting. There would always be an air of superiority about the victor dog, and an air of surliness about the conquered dog, and perhaps even an occasional snarl, but they wouldn't fight again and each had a certain security in the knowledge.

Counsel for the Prosecution:

You have heard what you may consider rather bizarre
evidence on the question of the publican's cat, but this has
been necessary to establish the exact nature of the fatal
act.

Counsel for the Defence:

A picture has been presented of the publican as a dedicated man of business inadvertently involved in tragedy because of his affection for his cat. I suggest that on his own evidence the publican is largely responsible for what happened.

The Judge:

To prove murder it is not necessary that the person killed is in any way connected with the person who kills. For example, a man who fires a rifle into a crowded street and kills somebody is guilty of murder. In cases where there is no connection between the murderer and the victim, it is necessary to prove that the act which finally led to the death was in itself illicit.

Mick had lost his cat and was looking for it. It had wandered behind the bar, as was its wont in the course of the afternoon, and Mick had stopped work to feed it. He had taken a can of cat food from the bar refrigerator where he kept a large stock, and led the cat around to the enclosed laundry yard of the hotel where it was normally fed in daylight hours. Mick had emptied the contents of the can, a purplish matter guaranteed on the label not to be kangaroo meat, into the cat's dish, a plastic confection with 'Kitty' written in large letters on its side.

Mick had watched with satisfaction as the enormous tom had absorbed the contents of the can, then left it there to rest in the sun while he trotted back to the bar. The laundry yard was surrounded by a ten foot brick wall, designed to protect the hotel laundry from casual thieves, and even the redoubtable Mol could not get out except through the door into the hotel, to which Mick and Jenny kept the only keys.

Half an hour after he had fed the cat Mick went back to the laundry to let him out because he knew from experience that Mol would want to take a stroll in the grounds.

Mick's custom was to accompany the cat on its stroll, then take it back to the bedroom he and Jenny and Mol shared. At this time in the afternoon there were a lot of drunks leaving the hotel and Mick was anxious that Mol should not run the risk of being flattened under the erratic wheels of their cars.

But now he found the door of the laundry yard swinging open. His great loose face fell into folds of worry. He looked quickly around the laundry yard. No Mol. He felt in his pocket for the key. It was still there. He was sure he had locked the door. Surely Jenny wouldn't have opened it. And, if she had, she would have made sure that Mol was looked after. That was it perhaps; Jenny had taken Mol for his walk and perhaps put him to bed. Mick trotted off to look for Jenny.

He found her in the kitchen supervising the preparation of the evening meal in the hotel dining room. She was studying two large steaks she held in either hand.

'Have you seen Mol, Jenny?' asked Mick.

'No, dear, not for an hour or two.' Jenny's round, fatuous face looked affectionately into her husband's. 'But don't worry about him, dear. He'll be all right.'

'Did you let him out of the laundry yard?'

'No, dear.'

'Well, I locked him in there a while ago after I fed him and now the door's open and he's gone.'

Distress and guilt filled the plump folds of Jenny's face.

'Oh, dear,' she said.

'What is it?' said Mick quickly.

'Oh, Mick,' she said sorrowfully. 'I gave the key of the laundry yard to Mary. There were some towels there I wanted. Mick, she must have let him out.'

'Damn,' said Mick. 'If that little bitch has let the cat out I'll have her out of here in five minutes.'

'Oh, Mick,' said Jenny justly. 'It wasn't her fault. She wouldn't know.' Then realizing that the tone of the conversation was more dramatic than the circumstances warranted. 'Anyway, Mick, you old goose, he'll be all right. He spends most of his time wandering around by himself.'

'You know I like him kept in on Saturday afternoons with all these bloody drunks around,' said Mick, coming as near as he ever did to reproving Jenny.

Jenny looked chastened for a moment, then smiled comfortingly. 'Anyhow I'll go and find him in a minute and put him to bed. Listen, dear, what do you think about these steaks?' she said, holding up the two pieces of meat. 'They've been in the meat drawer for a week, but I think they're all right.'

Mick conscientiously put his nose up against the meat and smelled it.

'It's all right,' he said, 'but use it in the Steak Diane.' Mick kept a reasonably good table. Those of his customers who ate in the dining room, he argued, were of a more discerning class than the young drunks who provided most of his income. The diners were also more likely to complain to some effect.

Jenny held the meat to her own button nose and wrinkled her face, wondering whether the pungent Diane sauce would do the trick.

'She'll be right, Jenny,' said Mick impatiently, 'now leave it and help me find Mol.'

It was Harris who first saw Peter squatting naked and, at a distance, faun-like, between the legs of the recumbent girl.

'Jesus Christ, look at that,' said Harris.

The two meatworkers looked down the slope into the little grove some fifty yards away where Peter was still contemplating his problem.

Verdon, whom Peter had most irritated by his appearance, was first to recognize him, mainly by the long, beautiful hair.

'It's that fuckin' little poofter,' he said.

Glad of some diversion from the humiliation they had just undergone, the two young men spontaneously turned down the slope. There were bell-birds in the scrub and their bright little notes penetrated the rolling stream of sound from the band in the hotel.

Peter had no idea of their presence until Verdon grabbed him by the hair and hurled him over on his back. Peter let out a howl which penetrated the girl's clouded brain and she began to stir.

'What's wrong with the bird?' said Harris. 'Has she been fucked silly?'

'Not with what he's got to fuck with,' said Verdon. 'What's she got that helmet on for?'

'Like a bag over the head. She must be a dog,' said Harris, kneeling beside the girl and beginning to undo the helmet. The girl rolled over and began waving her arms.

'Leave it on,' said Verdon. 'Who wants to see her fuckin' face?'

The two of them studied the girl, Harris with considerable lasciviousness, Verdon, experiencing a different emotion.

Peter grabbed his jeans and, unnoticed, slipped away into the scrub.

'She's pissed,' said Harris.

Verdon remembered Peter and turned around, but Peter was gone.

'Dirty little poofter must have been fiddling with her,' he said.

Harris ran an exploratory hand down the girl's body.

'Shame to waste a bird,' he said, looking up at Verdon.

'Well, go on, mate,' said Verdon generously. 'I'll keep watch.'

'Sure you wouldn't like to go first,' said Harris, in natural deference to a superior male.

But Verdon, by virtue of the beating he'd just taken and his earlier session with the prostitute, didn't feel all that capable. It was unthinkable that he should be seen to try and not succeed, so he retreated behind generosity again.

'No. You go on, mate.'

Gratefully accepting, Harris pulled down his jeans, forgetting that he couldn't get the tight trousers over his shoes. He had to sit down to take his shoes off. He too was of the no underpants persuasion and became aware as Peter had that a sand bed is not suitable for fornication or rape.

Finally trouserless, shoeless, but failing to discard his shirt, he lowered himself on to the girl. She was half conscious now and vomiting quietly behind the helmet.

'Come on, girlie,' he said, grasping her by the buttocks and trying to raise her pelvis.

Peter, circling back to try to retrieve his shirt, watched from a clump of bushes ten yards away. Even in his grief and envy he realized that he had something to learn here.

'Come on, girlie,' said Harris again, finding he couldn't get the girl's pelvis arched to the proper angle.

'You need a pillow,' said Verdon considerately, and gathering up the clothing scattered around the grove, folded it into a bundle and helped Harris stuff it under the girl's buttocks.

Peter frowned as he saw his beautiful shirt being maltreated. Harris found he could manage in principle now, but he'd struck another difficulty.

'Christ, she's tight, Johnny,' he grunted.

'Keep at it, mate, want a push?' said Verdon, grinning.

'Fuck off,' said Harris amiably.

He kept working for a while, but didn't make much progress.

'Can't get in,' he muttered bemusedly, pulling back to rest.

'Here I'll jack her up a bit,' said Verdon. He extricated the clothing from under the girl's body and doubled it over so that it made a larger ball.

'Try now,' he said, as he raised the girl with one hand under her buttocks and thrust the clothing back in place.

Harris went down on the girl again and after considerable effort found happening what he expected to happen.

'Christ, what a rotten fuck,' he said as he withdrew. Neither he nor Verdon had any experience in the deflowering of virgins.

'Have a go, Johnny,' said Harris, dusting the sand off his buttocks. 'See if you can do any better.' There was a certain flattery in the implication.

'Ah, fuck it, I'd sooner have a drink. Come on.' Verdon had enjoyed the spectacle but was not quite certain he had the capacity to emulate Harris.

'It's a shame to waste her, Johnny,' expostulated Harris, then seeing the reasonableness of Verdon's position, 'Mind you, she's no fuckin' good.'

He retrieved his jeans by jerking them out of the clothing under the girl so that she rolled over on to her face.

'Come on,' said Verdon.

'Hold it,' said Harris laughing, hopping after Verdon. 'Wait till I get me strides on.'

Peter watched them go, Harris pulling on his jeans as he went, clutching his shoes in one hand.

'What about the girl?' said Harris as they left the grove.

'Fuck her,' said Verdon.

'I just did,' said Harris and that kept them both laughing until they reached the hotel.

Peter crept back into the grove after a few minutes. He had some notion of renewing his attentions to the girl, but mostly he wanted to retrieve his shirt. The girl was writhing in the sand, clutching at the helmet as though she were trying to drag it off.

Peter untangled his shirt from her clothing and shook the sand out of it. It wasn't damaged and he slipped into it.

'Are you all right?' he said to the girl.

She moaned.

Peter knelt down and managed to undo the strap of the helmet. The girl's hands plucked at him, but he persisted because, after all, he had to get his helmet back. When he saw her vomit-stained face he abandoned his sexual aspirations and stood up, shaking his helmet to clear it of fluid.

'You'd better get dressed,' he said to the girl.

She looked blearily up at him and began to cry.

Peter wanted above all things now to get away, get back to security and the sound of the hotel, to the atmosphere of hope rather than actuality. The girl's naked, spattered body no longer attracted him. He felt vaguely annoyed that she'd done better by the other bloke than she had by him. But as her sobbing became louder he was moved by an impulse of kindness.

'I'll give you a hand,' he said.

He shook out her rumpled blouse and guided her arms into the sleeves. As he did up the buttons his hands encountered her breasts and he felt desire again, but that was quickly extinguished when she vomited copiously.

'Careful,' he said, moving away to protect his shirt.

He tried to get her jeans on but she began screaming when she felt his hands on her legs.

'Hey, cut it out,' said Peter. 'I'm only trying to help.'

But the girl kept on screaming, loud, hopeless animal screams.

Peter gave up trying to be kind, grabbed his helmet and bolted up the slope towards his motor-bike.

He would have driven home except that there was nothing there for him, and anyway, for the first time in his young life, he felt he wanted a drink, rather than that he ought to have one.

As he parked his bike in the hotel car park he saw Mick dodging among the parked cars.

'Here, puss, puss, puss,' Mick was calling in a high falsetto tone. 'Here, puss, puss, puss. Where are you, Mol? Mol. Can you hear me? Here, puss, puss, puss.'

Peter went into the lounge bar and ordered a glass of beer. All the tables were taken now so he stood at the bar to drink.

Verdon and Harris were at the other end of the bar and didn't see him. Peter hadn't given them any more thought. They'd chased him away from the bird and that was that. In fact he felt about Verdon much as Verdon felt about the man who'd beaten him up. Verdon's attitude to Peter was by no means the same. Verdon was feeling bad, and even the beer he was pouring down now didn't do anything to alleviate the feeling. It wasn't the pain of his wounds; physical pain did not affect him greatly, but it was sinking into him that he'd suffered three major defeats that afternoon. He'd had to pay for a woman (the fact that his mate had made the actual payment made no difference); he'd been thrashed badly in a fight; and he'd stood over a naked girl and known that he could do nothing about it. Somehow the balance of things was upset and the way to redress that balance was to demolish someone. His mate Harris was out of the question, the man who'd beaten him would beat him again, and even now he knew he wasn't capable of another woman.

So when he saw Peter at the other end of the bar his frustration crystallized into a visual form.

'There's that fuckin' poofter again,' he said to Harris. It would be absurd to suggest that Verdon thought, but somehow in his very nearly pickled brain, the link was forged between Peter and his misfortunes. It was the poofter who'd picked up the girl Verdon had first approached; if it hadn't been for that he wouldn't have had to go with the tart; and if he hadn't gone off with the tart he wouldn't have had the fight; and, Christ Almighty, it had been the poofter in the grove with the naked girl.

'I'm gonna kill that little cunt,' he said.

'Have another drink,' said Harris peaceably. Harris was feeling all right. He was full of beer, he'd had a screw and he'd done the right thing by his mate, bought him out of a lot of trouble. Harris didn't even want his five dollars back. He felt even more warmly than usual towards Verdon because, for a change, he didn't feel particularly inferior to him.

'I'm gonna kill him,' said Verdon.

'Don't go starting trouble in the bar,' said Harris. 'They'll only throw you out. Wait till later.'

That was reasonable, Verdon acknowledged, and turned to his beer again. He felt better now that he knew what was troubling him. He was dimly aware that Harris was patronizing him, or aware of a change in their relationship, but that had to do with the little poofter too and all would be rectified when he smashed the bastard.

'Keep an eye on him,' he said to Harris. 'I'll take him as soon as he leaves.'

'All right, mate,' said Harris. 'Two more beers, Mick.'

Mick served the beer absently, although with his usual lightning efficiency. He still hadn't found Mol. He'd tackled Mary, the temporary waitress, and she'd admitted that the cat had escaped from the laundry yard when she'd opened the door.

'But I couldn't help it, Mick,' she said, aghast at the trembling mass of rage that confronted her. 'He just shot out when I opened the door.'

'Then why didn't you tell me, you stupid little bitch!'

said Mick, tempted almost to strike her. 'Anyhow, drop whatever you're doing and find him.'

'All right, Mick,' said the girl. 'I'll find him.'

'You'd better and do it quick, because I'm docking the time you spend looking off your pay.'

The girl didn't resent this because she felt terribly guilty about the cat and was inclined to respect Mick's deep affection.

She'd now spent the past hour scouring the hotel and the grounds, but with no sign of Mol.

'Still no sign of Mol,' Mick said worriedly to Jenny as she came bustling past him.

'I know, dear, I know,' said Jenny, biting her lip. 'I'm that worried. But if anything had happened we'd have heard, don't you think?'

'I don't know. I suppose so,' said Mick, thinking how anonymous were those bundles of blood and fur on the highway each morning, mute evidence of the inability of cats to cope with the increasing night traffic.

But he didn't say anything to Jenny because he could see that she was getting really upset now.

There was a disturbance in the foyer of the hotel. A crowd of youths had gathered there, laughing and shouting. Other youths were pushing away from their tables and rushing to the foyer.

Mick grabbed his ebony baton and trotted around the bar. It didn't sound like a fight; the shouts lacked the deep exultation that went with a fight, but any unusual gathering in the hotel was a danger to the furniture and Mick, the good shepherd, would protect hotel property with his person if necessary.

He pushed roughly through the crowd and found himself facing a young girl, naked except for a thin blouse half-undone. She was clutching a pair of jeans in some vague attempt to cover herself and she was sobbing into the faces of the laughing crowd.

Mick for once was slightly out of countenance. He looked around for Jenny, but she was out of sight behind the bar.

'Now come on, break it up. Break it up,' he said, automatically pushing at the chests of the nearest youths. 'Go on back to the bar.' Then he took the sobbing girl by the shoulder and propelled her towards the female toilets.

'You just go in there and put your trousers on,' he said. 'Come along now. Go in there and put your trousers on. You can't run around the hotel like that.'

The girl moved while he pushed, but as soon as he took his hand away she stopped, and stood there, clutching her jeans, tears cutting little clean lines down her soiled cheeks.

'Come along, girlie,' said Mick. 'You go in there and put your trousers on.'

Mick realized that another young girl was pushing with both hands against his stomach.

'Now cut that out,' he said. 'Go along, get back to the bar.'

'Let her alone, you bastard, can't you see she's been done over? Call the cops, you bastard.'

Mick looked down at the screaming girl. She had two companions. All were glaring at him, and two of them were plucking at the hand with which he held the crying girl's shoulder.

'Let her alone, you bastard. Call the cops and get her a doctor.'

Mick made a decision.

'You know her, do you?'

'Course we know her. She came with us. Now get her a bloody doctor.'

Mick opened his arms wide and sweeping the four girls

before him moved towards the hotel doors.

'No. You just take her home and see she's all right. Understand. It's got nothing to do with the hotel. It must have happened outside. Now you put her clothes on and take her home. Come along, no trouble now.'

Irresistibly Mick's bulk pushed the girls out through the doors to the cheers and laughter of the mob of young people who still crowded the foyer.

One of the girls kicked at Mick's legs, but it was like a mouse attacking a draught horse.

'You rotten bastard, can't you see she's been raped!' the girl screamed.

'Yes, well we don't want any trouble, so you just take her along home and see she's all right,' said Mick, thrusting the girl through the doorway and beginning to pull the doors shut.

The girl who kicked Mick was persistent. What's more she'd caught sight of Peter who'd joined the onlookers.

'She's been raped I tell you,' as Mick dislodged her clinging fingers from the door. 'She's been raped and there's the bastard that did it.'

She let go the doorway to point at Peter, who was quite close to Mick. Mick took advantage of the situation to push her arm outside and shut the door. He put the bolts in place. This was his standard method of solving problems. He knew the girls would mill around outside for a few minutes and consider coming back by another entrance, but they'd almost certainly just fade away.

He took no notice of the last accusation by the screaming girl, but Peter brought doom on himself.

'It wasn't me, Mick,' he gabbled, grabbing at Mick's arm. 'It wasn't me. It was two other blokes, Mick. Honest. I'll point 'em to you. They're in the bar now.'

Mick wasn't at all interested and simply shepherded Peter

along with the rest of the crowd back towards the bar.

But Verdon and Harris, who had also joined the crowd in the foyer, were interested.

'I'll point 'em out to you, Mick, and the girl will tell you it was them,' Peter rambled.

'Nothing to do with the hotel,' muttered Mick ritually, 'nothing to do with the hotel. Now come along back inside and settle down. Come along now.'

The girls were banging on the doors and Mick was wondering whether to go out and chase them further away. Better not. They'd quieten down in a minute.

The crowd in the foyer had thinned and Mick brushed past the boy who was clutching at his arm and went through to the lounge bar to get the band going.

Peter was left almost face to face with Verdon and Harris.

Counsel for the Defence:

It is on what you believe happened then and why it happened that you will bring in your verdict.

If the evidence of Verdon and his friends is to be believed, and I suggest it must be, then they held the youth Watts because they believed him guilty of rape. Because of the disinclination of the publican to take action they took it upon themselves to apprehend the youth and call for the police. It is reasonable to suppose that they honestly held their opinion : they say they had seen the youth by the beach with the naked, unconscious girl; they had heard the girl's friends accuse him; they say he admitted the act when challenged.

If Verdon was right his action was justified, and Watts was in fact attempting to escape from lawful custody.

Counsel for the Prosecution:

You may wonder, ladies and gentleman, why only one man is charged with murder when the prosecution's case, if established, would necessarily implicate three others at least as accessories. This however is a technicality of Law which is no concern of yours in arriving at your verdict. Whatever results flow from your verdict is equally a matter of no concern to you. It may be that other charges would result from whatever verdict you arrive at. That is no concern of yours.

All you must do is decide on the facts presented to you whether or not you accept the defence's position on the actions of Verdon or whether you accept, I suggest, the more probable version that Verdon attacked Watts in a homicidal frenzy.

If Verdon attacked Watts in a homicidal frenzy then Verdon is guilty of murder, even though he did not kill Watts.

The Judge:

Provided the accused was recklessly indifferent to human life, or provided that he had the intention to kill someone, it is immaterial that he had no particular victim in view. It is similarly immaterial if he kills the wrong person because of a mistake or miscarriage of his original plans. Equally, if as a result of an illicit action someone is killed, then the perpetrator of that illicit action is guilty of murder.

With one impulse Verdon and Harris pushed Peter to the other side of the hotel foyer, then grabbed him and dragged him up the stairs. A few of the youths saw them go, assumed that Peter was going to be bashed and turned and went back to their drinks. If the bashing had been public they would have stood and watched, but as it was it had nothing to do with them. Verdon and Harris didn't know where they were going; they just wanted to get away from where a disturbance would bring Mick and his baton. One of the bedroom doors on the first floor was open and they pushed Peter in there.

He hadn't thought to yell as yet, but as soon as he saw Verdon close and lock the door he let out a terrible scream. Verdon stopped it by hitting him in the mouth. He needn't have bothered; the band was going again now and a cannon could have been fired in the hotel without being noticed twenty feet away.

Peter sat down on the floor and looked up at the two men fearfully.

'Shit, look at it,' said Verdon. 'Look at it, Bob.'

Harris looked.

'Hard to believe, isn't it, Johnny?' said Harris.

'And this was gonna point us out to the cops. Weren't you, matie?'

Peter, who sensed that he was in real trouble, said nothing.

'Look at the shirt it's wearing,' said Verdon.

'Pretty,' said Harris.

'I reckon we ought to cut him,' said Verdon.

'Don't suppose he's got anything to cut,' said Harris and giggled at his own wit.

'Maybe not. Maybe he's got tits.'

Verdon leaned down and ripped at Peter's shirt. It was stout material and Peter was hauled backwards and forwards across the floor a few times before it came away in Verdon's hand.

Peter instinctively crossed his arms over his frail bony chest and Verdon and Harris were convulsed with laughter.

'Christ, mate, you were right,' said Harris.

'Let's see if he's got any balls,' said Verdon and grabbed at Peter's belt. The belt was very stout and Peter found himself hauled bodily into the air.

'You got a knife?' said Verdon.

Harris felt in his pockets and came up with a heavy pocket knife. He levered out the blade and handed it to Verdon.

Verdon dropped Peter on the floor, roughly thrust the knife under his belt and slashed.

'Better keep still, poofter, or you'll lose the little you've got,' said Verdon. Peter lay on the floor and shivered as Verdon hacked and slashed at his jeans finally ripping away most of the trunk without inflicting more damage than one slash on Peter's buttocks.

Naked to the loins, his jeans in tatters around his thighs, Peter lay on his back and looked up at his tormentors.

'Please,' he mumbled.

They laughed.

'Please,' said Verdon. 'Please, he says, please.'

'What do you say I cut him?' said Verdon, kneeling down suddenly and pushing the blade of the knife under Peter's scrotum.

Peter screamed as he felt the blade on his flesh, but he

didn't dare move.

Verdon began sawing the blade backwards and forwards, not enough to cut deeply, but enough to draw blood.

'Oh, please. Oh Christ, please!' screamed Peter.

'Please, he says, please,' said Verdon. 'See, Bob, he wants me to do it.'

Harris swayed back on his heels and laughed. Johnny was a mad bastard. He probably would cut the little bugger too. But Verdon had an idea. He couldn't formulate why he wanted it, but he wanted the demolition of Peter to be more public. If possible he would have liked the man who had beaten him up to be present, or even the bird Bob had screwed by the beach; but failing them he just wanted more people.

He rocked back on his haunches.

'Duck down to the bar and get a couple of the blokes,' he said. 'We'll have a bit of fun here.'

'Couple of the blokes?' said Harris, whose psyche wasn't nearly as complicated as Verdon's.

'Yeah. I got an idea. Got an idea for a bit of fun. We'll try this bastard.'

'Try him?' said Harris, amiably but bemusedly.

'Yeah. We oughta fix him, but it ought to be done proper. Go and get a couple of the blokes.'

'All right, Johnny,' said Harris. Johnny was a mad bastard but if he wanted a couple of blokes, he wanted a couple of blokes. Knowing Johnny it would probably be worthwhile.

'And, Bob,' said Verdon, as an afterthought, 'get a couple of bottles of whisky.' Verdon pulled ten dollars out of his pocket.

'That'll be right, Johnny,' said Harris. 'I got plenty.'

'Nah, take it,' said Verdon. 'I owe you five anyway.' It

was the first time he had felt able to refer to the debt.

Harris shrugged and took the money and went down to the bar to find some blokes.

Mary had found Mol.

She had spent the past hour and a half searching the hotel, through all the guest rooms, the kitchen, the dining room, all around the grounds, the female toilets, the male toilets by proxy of one of the barmen and at last she'd found him in the car park.

The great tom was stalking a pair of seagulls searching among the scraps of pies and sandwiches littering the ground. He was crouching beside a rubbish bin, his bushy tail slowly waving to and fro as his feral eyes stared at the gulls.

His shoulders low, he cautiously went forward another few inches, then stopped, still, powerful, lethal.

Mary picked him up.

With a growl he slashed at her wrist. She dropped him and seeing the lines of blood welling on her skin forgot the surge of relief she'd felt at finding him and let fly a kick with her pointed shoe.

The toe sank into the tom's well-covered side and he screeched and bounded away across the car park straight under the wheels of a backing car.

Mol howled, the car horn blew, Mary screamed.

Mol flung himself from under the car and tried to flee, but a broken hind leg crumpled under him and he rolled over. Spitting and growling he dragged himself to the lone tree in the car park and hauled himself up by the front legs until he was twenty feet from the ground. There he sat, alternately growling and worrying at the leg that hung so limply and uselessly.

Terrified and conscience-stricken, Mary ran to find Mick.

Harris came back with two blokes, sodden young louts who had been lured up to the room by a promise of some fun and a share of the two bottles of whisky Harris was carrying. They too were meatworkers but merely general hands on the floor, of a much lower social order than either Harris or Verdon. They knew the other two slightly and had in fact on a couple of occasions joined them in a fracas when the meatworkers had come into collision with a group of water-skiers or bikies.

Now they felt, inasmuch as they were capable of feeling anything, that they were rallying again to the call of their mates, quite apart from the matter of the whisky.

They looked solemnly at the almost naked, tear-stained Peter, but they were past any sensation of surprise.

'Come in,' said Verdon, hospitably. 'Have a drink.'

They could find only two glasses in the room so Harris filled these for the two newcomers and he and Verdon drank straight from the bottles.

'Sit down, fellas,' said Verdon, indicating the twin beds in the room. Solemnly the other three sat down and Verdon, bottle in one hand and open knife in the other, stood near Peter's head.

'Now why I asked you up here,' he said, slurring his words badly but still quite comprehensible, 'was to see a fair go.'

His audience nodded sagely.

'Y'see this little turd here,' he stirred Peter with the point of his boot, 'gives me the shits.'

They all looked down at the offending Peter.

'And I'm going to take the shit out of him,' continued Verdon, 'but I just wanted to make sure I was right. And I want you fellas to say whether you think I'm right or not. Y'see?'

Again they all nodded. It seemed eminently reasonable.

Verdon swayed and took another drink, trying to re-assemble his thoughts. He was finding it hard to remember why he loathed Peter. He knew he did and that was enough for him, but he'd put himself in the position of having to explain his loathing in words and he found his mind suddenly seemed blank.

'But you see what I mean,' he said to the group. 'I mean I wouldn't want to tear shit out of him if you blokes didn't think I should.'

The blokes nodded.

'So I'm gonna tell you why ... that's what I'm going to do ... I'm going to tell you why.'

'Good on you, Johnny,' said Harris loyally.

'And this is why ... this is why,' Verdon stopped again, shaking his head.

There was a long pause.

'Well, look at the fucker's hair,' shouted Verdon suddenly. 'Look at it ... I mean I ask you ... he's a fuckin' poofter ...'

The other three looked with distaste at the deviate.

Verdon had found his line of thought now.

'And do you know ... do you know, Bob here and me, we found this bloody little poofter down on the beach fiddling with a bird. Fiddling with a bird. Couldn't even root her. Had to fiddle with her.'

The disgust grew on the faces of the three seated men.

'Give us another drink, Bob,' said one.

Verdon swayed again, a puzzled expression on his face. There was something else, surely there was something else.

It was not an easily embarrassed audience, but the pause was prolonged.

'And he wanted to dob us in to the cops, Johnny,' prompted Harris.

'That's right,' roared Verdon triumphantly. 'He wanted to dob us in to the cops. This little shit wanted to dob us in to the cops. Well, Jesus Christ, I ask you . . .'

'Bastard,' said one of the newcomers.

'Stinking rotten poofter bastard,' said the other.

'Well, what would you do, eh? I ask you, what would you do if you were me?'

That puzzled them. They were quite willing to agree with anything Verdon might want to do, but it was too much to expect them to make a suggestion.

'Well, I'm gonna cut his balls out,' said Verdon, explanatorily, a reasonable man taking the only possible course.

As the others nodded their assent to the justice of the proposition a light grew in the alcohol-dimmed eyes of Verdon.

'No, I'm not. Oh, Jesus Christ,' he said fervently, 'no, I'm not. Bob, mate . . . Bob, go and get me a hammer.'

'Here, puss, puss, puss,' called Mick distractedly. 'Here, puss, puss, puss.'

Mol crouched on the branch of the tree and spat at his master.

The distraught Mick could see the broken limb dangling. He knew the sickness of seeing a loved creature in pain.

'Go and get the extension ladder,' Mick snapped at one of the two barmen he had seconded to help with the rescue despite the detriment to the bar trade.

'Come on down, Mol,' pleaded Mick. 'Dad won't hurt you. Come on, Mol. We'll get you to a doctor and you'll be right, old boy. Come on down, Mol.'

The cat spat.

The barman came back with the extension ladder and set

it up against the tree. The top reached within a few yards of the wounded Mol.

'I'll go and get him, Mick,' said the barman.

'No,' said Mick. 'He wouldn't let you handle him.'

Mick weighed eighteen stone, the ladder seemed frail and the penalties of a fall of ten or fifteen feet would be heavy, but Mick didn't give them a thought in his concern for his pet.

With the two barmen holding the shaking ladder, he mounted quickly and extended a hand to the snarling Mol.

'Come on, Mol. Come to dad. Come on, old boy. I'll look after you.'

The cat spat and struck with its claws at its master's hands.

'The poor old boy's hysterical,' said Mick. 'Pass me up a bag or something.'

'You'd better come down, Mick, while I get it. It needs two of us to hold this with you on it.'

'No. You get a bag. I'll stay here and try to calm him.'

Perched high on the creaking and shifting ladder Mick extended his loving hands to the cat and murmured soothing words.

Harris wandered irresolutely into the bar. If Johnny wanted a hammer he would have one if it were within Harris's power, but he didn't know where he would get one.

He breasted the bar and said to the young barman, 'Could you lend us a hammer, mate?'

'Eh?' said the barman.

'Could you lend us a hammer?'

'A hammer?'

'Yeah, a hammer, you know a hammer.'

'No, mate,' said the barman briskly, 'sorry, can't help you.'

Harris went out into the car yard and pulled at the boots of a few cars. Some came open but he could find no hammer. There was knot of people at the other end of the car park and Harris recognized the huge bulk of Mick apparently suspended in a tree. He drifted over to the group.

'Here, puss, puss, puss,' Mick was saying. 'Come on, Mol. Come to dad.'

Harris, unsurprised, looked up at Mick.

'Hey, Mick,' he said. 'Have you got a hammer you could lend us?'

Mick, intent on rescuing Mol, did not hear him, and certainly would not have replied if he had.

Harris gave up. He went back into the hotel, up the stairs and into the room where Verdon was waiting for the hammer. Peter was still lying on the floor with Verdon standing over him. The other two were sitting on one of the beds with glasses of whisky in their hands.

'Can't find a hammer anywhere, Johnny,' said Harris.

Verdon, who was still swigging neat whisky from the bottle, had almost forgotten about the hammer, but now that Harris reminded him he remembered his strange purpose.

He cast about the room and observed that the beds were made of iron and, if disassembled, might yield an iron pole that would be suitable to his ends.

'Help us get this bed apart,' he said, dragging the mattress on to the floor.

The other three obligingly tried to help him, but the simple mechanics were too much for their disorientated limbs.

'What do you want anyway, Johnny,' said Harris at length.

'I want something to beat this little bastard's head in with,' said Verdon.

'Why not just use your boots?' said Harris practically.

Verdon thought about that.

'No,' he said finally. 'I want to do it proper.' Dimly it seemed to him that the use of a hammer, or a reasonable substitute, would make the demolition of Peter more an execution than a bashing.

One of the other meatworkers had been pondering the problem.

'Listen,' he said. 'I got a jack in me car. Would that do?'

Verdon considered.

'Yeah,' he said. 'A jack'd be good. Go and get it.'

The meatworker lumbered out of the room.

'Wish you'd said that before,' said Harris. 'I could of got a jack.'

Verdon ignored him.

Peter, stirred by the sheer horror of what was about to happen to him, made a dive to follow the meatworker out of the door, but Verdon kicked him heavily in the ribs as he went past on his hands and knees. Peter was flung against the wall and lay with his eyes bulging, making little whooping noises as he tried to get air back into his lungs. The meatworker came back in a few minutes with the car jack and handed it to Verdon. Verdon swung it over his shoulder in his classical style and grunted disapprovingly. It was all wrong, the balance didn't feel good, but it would have to do.

'All right,' he said. 'Now I'll get up here and you drive the poofter past me.' He stepped on to the bed which still had its mattress in place and he stood there precariously, finding it difficult to keep his balance on the yielding material.

Owlishly the other three regarded him. It was Harris who first got the idea.

'I get ya, Johnny.' He walked over to Peter. 'You get up and run past that bed,' he said.

Peter curled up against the wall and squealed.

Harris picked him up and tried to push him towards Verdon who was swaying on the mattress, swinging the jack in one hand.

Peter pulled away and bolted to the door. One of the other meatworkers caught him and pushed him back.

'I'll lead him past you, Johnny,' said Harris.

Peter tried to scramble away on his hands and knees and Harris grabbed him by the hair and tried to pull him past the bed below Verdon. When the wriggling, sobbing boy was within range Verdon swung the jack, but Peter pulled away, Verdon overbalanced and the jack went very near to landing on Harris's head.

'Christ,' said Harris. 'Easy, Johnny.'

The other two meatworkers were finding the whole situation confusing and contented themselves with leaning against the door, effectively preventing any possibility of Peter's escape.

Verdon climbed back on to the bed and found he'd forgotten the jack which he'd dropped when he fell.

'Give us the jack,' he said to Harris.

Harris let go of Peter to bend down for the jack. Peter leaped across to the window and tried to open it. Harris went after him, but Peter was by far the soberest person in the room by now and he dodged Harris. He found himself in the middle of the room, hedged in by Harris, Verdon and the two meatworkers for all the world like an hysterical steer being driven to the slaughter, or an hysterical calf.

He opened his mouth and screamed and screamed until Harris lurched across and hit him in the back of the neck. Peter fell down.

Harris picked up the jack and handed it to Verdon.

'Get him along here,' said Verdon.

Harris picked up Peter and shook him. The boy was conscious but in a state of total collapse from fear and shock.

'Need the pole, Johnny,' said Harris, referring to the electric rod with which recalcitrant beasts were urged into the killing pen.

On the bedside table of the hotel room was a reading lamp connected to the power with lengths of flex about two yards long. Verdon stared at one of these, trying to work out some method of using it to prod Peter into going to the slaughter more co-operatively. But the notion was too complex and he abandoned it. He could easily have walked over to Peter and beaten his brains out as he sat sobbing on the floor, but for some reason the notion of ritual was strong within him and he wanted to swing the jack down from a height as was his custom in the killing pen.

'Hey, you two,' he said to the meatworkers against the door, 'give Johnny a hand to lead the little bastard over here.'

It was doubtful whether these two realized they were party to any more than a thorough beating up, and they co-operatively left the doorway and laid hands on Peter.

'That's right,' said Verdon. 'Now just lead him up here where I can get a good swing at him.'

Mol wasn't remotely interested in getting into the bag Mick held out towards him. He had retreated further up the slender limb and was glaring at his master, giving pain to Mick's heart because his cat so obviously blamed him for the pain and distress it was feeling.

'Come on, Mol,' he said, coaxing, patient. 'Come on here. I'll get you down.' In his innermost soul Mick dreaded what he had to do, because he could see that the cat's leg was badly broken and bundling the animal into the bag and bearing it away to a veterinary surgeon could only make things immediately worse. But what else was a man to do?

He called down to the men holding the ladder.

'One of you go and ring the vet and tell him to get out here as quick as he can.'

Then doubt attacked him. What if he managed to rescue Mol in the next few minutes? He would have to wait for the vet. It might be better if he could rush Mol off by car immediately.

'No. Wait on,' he called. 'Let's see if I can get him.'

Jenny, her round little face tear-stained and fearful, looked up at her husband and the cat.

'Be careful, Mick,' she pleaded.

'I'm being careful,' said Mick irritably, wobbling dangerously as he stretched even further to reach Mol. 'This bloody ladder's in the wrong place, we'll have to move it.'

He clambered down the ladder and moved it to a spot directly under Mol.

'Let me go up, Mick,' said one of the barmen again. 'I'm lighter than you.'

'I'll do it,' said Mick shortly, and went up the ladder again.

The ladder was about three feet short and Mick precariously climbed as far as he could, then stood up swaying dangerously for a moment until he grasped a branch of the tree. Then he climbed the next couple of steps and was standing on the very top of the ladder, one hand holding the branch and the other the bag.

At last he was within easy reach of Mol.

He stretched the bag out and Mol ungratefully slashed at his hand.

'There, there, Mol,' said Mick, disregarding the streaks of blood and the stinging pain. 'There, there, old fellow.'

He lunged at the cat with the bag; his foot slipped on the ladder and he hung, one foot in the air, one on the ladder, the branch of the tree plunging under his weight. The cat snarled. Jenny screamed and threw her considerable weight into helping the barmen keep the ladder steady. Mick dropped the bag and grabbed the branch with both hands. His groping foot found the ladder but he could not balance himself and he hung there, feet on the ladder, hands on the tree, leaning out into space with little apparent hope of ever being able to move again.

Verdon raised the jack as the other men led Peter towards him.

'Go easy with that, Johnny,' said Harris, no longer greatly confident in the accuracy of Verdon's aim.

Peter stared incredulously into the sodden face of the man who was standing on the bed, weapon in hand, intending to kill him.

He screamed and struggled and shook his head from side to side.

Verdon raised the jack higher. He couldn't get a proper swing so he'd just bring it straight down on the little bastard's head.

Peter began to kick, raising both feet from the ground and threshing frantically. But his slight weight made no impression on the meatworkers and they bore him inexorably forward.

As he came in range Verdon brought the jack down.

Peter screamed and convulsed his body. Verdon staggered slightly as he struck. The jack hit one of the meatworkers and neatly broke his collar bone.

The man roared and released his hold on Peter.

Peter squirmed away from the other meatworker and, seeing the jack dangling in front of his eyes as Verdon struggled to regain balance, grabbed it. Verdon came tumbling down on the floor and Peter for a moment was free with the jack in his hand. Desperately he swung it but hit nobody. He made for the door but there was someone in front of him. He turned and darted to the window, throwing the jack at it as he went. The jack went through the window, shattering the glass and spun out into the night. Peter went after it.

Peter came tumbling out of the window into the upper branches of the tree a few feet above Mick, still suspended between the ladder and the branch.

Peter clutched at the thin branches and fell, straight down on Mick. Mick, assailed almost simultaneously by the jack, a shower of glass and the flailing screaming boy, released his hold. He crashed down on Jenny, all eighteen stone of him, and broke her neck.

Counsel for the Defence:

Irrespective of what views you come to regarding the facts of this case, consider once more some of the elements required to prove murder:

The death of a human being,
That the act of the accused caused the death of a human being,
That the act was done with reckless indifference to human life.

And consider whether the act of selling alcohol to a man who is already drunk could reasonably be held to be murder when that act leads to the death of a human being.

The only truth that has emerged from this trial is that the publican murdered his wife.

David Morell
Testament 75p

Reuben Bourne, a freelance journalist publishes an interview that exposes a fanatical underground network that is ready and able to kill anyone on command . . .

Suddenly, *he* becomes their target — the police cannot help — his only hope is to take his family on a desperate scramble for the safety of open country.

'Terrors brilliantly told' SUNDAY TELEGRAPH

'A brilliant piece of sustained suspense'
MANCHESTER EVENING NEWS

David Morell
First Blood 60p

Bare-ass naked, Rambo roared out of Madison on a stolen motorbike. He left behind a trigger happy cop — spilling his guts on the cell floor . . .

Be-medalled Green Beret, Rambo had survived captivity and torture in Vietnam. Trained as an expert killer, he draws his pursuers into the hills — where he can fight back Guerrilla style !

'Brutal, Bloody, Violent, Profane and absolutely superb' OVER 21

'The most chilling story of a man hunt I have ever read'
DAILY EXPRESS

Colin Dexter
Last Seen Wearing 70p

Missing Teenager . . . Police Re-open Case — and the Valerie Taylor dossier landed on Inspector Morse's desk. There were all the usual leads — pot-smoking boyfriend, middle-aged schoolmasters, strip-clubs and abortion clinics — and they all led back to square one. The missing girl had spread her sexual favours wide and on this case Morse became the victim of temptation far beyond the call of duty.

Selected bestsellers

- ☐ **The Eagle Has Landed** Jack Higgins 80p
- ☐ **The Moneychangers** Arthur Hailey 95p
- ☐ **Marathon Man** William Goldman 70p
- ☐ **Nightwork** Irwin Shaw 75p
- ☐ **Tropic of Ruislip** Leslie Thomas 75p
- ☐ **One Flew Over The Cuckoo's Nest** Ken Kesey 75p
- ☐ **Collision** Spencer Dunmore 70p
- ☐ **Perdita's Prince** Jean Plaidy 70p
- ☐ **The Eye of the Tiger** Wilbur Smith 80p
- ☐ **The Shootist** Glendon Swarthout 60p
- ☐ **Of Human Bondage** Somerset Maugham 95p
- ☐ **Rebecca** Daphne du Maurier 80p
- ☐ **Slay Ride** Dick Francis 60p
- ☐ **Jaws** Peter Benchley 70p
- ☐ **Let Sleeping Vets Lie** James Herriot 60p
- ☐ **If Only They Could Talk** James Herriot 60p
- ☐ **It Shouldn't Happen to a Vet** James Herriot 60p
- ☐ **Vet In Harness** James Herriot 60p
- ☐ **Tinker Tailor Soldier Spy** John le Carré 75p
- ☐ **Gone with the Wind** Margaret Mitchell £1.75
- ☐ **Cashelmara** Susan Howatch £1.25
- ☐ **The Nonesuch** Georgette Heyer 60p
- ☐ **The Grapes of Wrath** John Steinbeck 95p
- ☐ **Drum** Kyle Onstott 60p

All these books are available at your bookshop or newsagent; or can be obtained direct from the publisher
Pan Books, Sales Office, Cavaye Place, London SW10 9PG
Just tick the titles you want and fill in the form below
Prices quoted are applicable in UK
Send purchase price plus 20p for the first book and 10p for each additional book, to allow for postage and packing

Name _____
(block letters please)
Address _____

_____

While every effort is made to keep prices low, it is sometimes necessary to increase prices at short notice. Pan Books reserve the right to show on covers new retail prices which may differ from those advertised in the text or elsewhere